LONDON SOUL

NANA MALONE

COPYRIGHT

This is a work of fiction. Names, characters, places, and incidents either are the product of the author's imagination or are used fictitiously, and any resemblance to actual persons living or dead, business establishments, events, or locales, is entirely coincidental.

London Soul

Cover Art by Staci Hart

Edited by Angie Ramey and Michele Ficht

Published in the United States of America

CHAPTER ONE

ABBIE

First rule of fighting assholes is kick first ask questions later.

Maybe Easton thought I was kidding.

Maybe he thought I really wouldn't fight back. Maybe he thought that, like all those years before, I would just give him what he wanted. But Easton didn't know me very well anymore.

Because I was going to fight for my life. Fight for my freedom. I knew what it meant now to have someone who actually cared about me. And I wasn't letting that go without a fight.

I kicked. I punched. I fought like hell. He reached for the black bag that was over my head, and I whipped my hand out. I didn't have enough leverage to really get proper punches in, but I was doing what I could. I wasn't going down without a fight. Not today.

I wasn't going to live in fear anymore.

I heard a voice say, "Jesus Christ! She's one hell of a fighter."

And then, another more familiar voice said, "Jesus! Just take it off so she knows she's not in danger."

I frowned. The voice was female. *Ilani?*

The black bag was removed from my head, and I raised my hands, ready to defend myself. I blinked rapidly to adjust to the light, and I saw Ilani peering at me. "Ilani? What the fuck?" Why wasn't she black bagged? Ilani whacked at the arm of someone and my gaze darted that way. *Dane, from class?* "What the fuck, you guys? Are you trying to sell me? I swear you'll get more for Ilani than you will for me."

There were two other guys and a mousy-haired brunette in the van with us. They were vaguely familiar. I knew their faces but couldn't place them. I stepped back, and Ilani held up her hands.

"Abbie, are you okay?"

I noted the open van door and a curious onlooker who jogged by. They'd parked on the far end of the park with less foot traffic, so if I was going to fight, I'd need to make a hell of a lot of noise. "Someone had better start fucking talking right now."

One of the other guys held up his hand. "Hey, I'm Jackson. I'm one of Xander's TAs."

The second guy waved at me. "Garreth. I finished the masters course last year."

The girl waved. "Madison. I'm his TA and sometimes his assistant for shoots."

Jackson darted his gaze to Garreth. "We're the Daylighters. You, Ilani, and Dane have been selected."

My gaze flickered to Ilani then to a ruddy-faced Dane. "Selected to what, win a free kidnapping? Can I decline this prize?"

Ilani snorted.

Jackson shook his head. "Right. I forgot. You don't know what the Daylighters are. It's kind of a secret society for photography and media students. They select three students a year. Surprise and welcome?" He grinned.

I scooted back as far as I could go until my back was up against the door of the van. "So, what, you just kidnap people off the street?"

Madison winced. "I told you lot watching too much of *The Skulls* was a bad idea. You've terrified her."

Garreth held up his hands. "Mate, don't blame me. Jackson wanted to go for maximum effect. I told you it wasn't a good idea. She looks jumpy."

Madison sighed. "Sorry about these idiots. When Jackson said they were going to grab you, I sincerely thought they meant pick you up. Not, you know, literally *grab* you. Normally, we wouldn't approach you cold, but you didn't reply to your invitation letter. We thought you knew about the Daylighters, present kidnapping situation not-with-standing."

I frowned. "Invitation letter?"

Ilani held up her invitation that was lettered in a gray embossed font. And then I thought back. I'd gotten a letter like that last week. I'd ignored it because it looked fancy, and so I assumed it was from Easton. "I need someone to do a better job of explaining."

Jackson did his best. "We take the best of Xander's

students, and they become Daylighters. The ones who help in his galleries. Occasionally, you get to exhibit, and we go out and shoot together. I know it sounds nerdy, but it's actually pretty wicked."

"So you guys couldn't just, you know, ask in class or something? 'Who wants to be in our secret club?' I could have tased you to death."

Garreth shrugged. "Well, it wouldn't exactly be a secret then, would it?"

My gaze flickered between Ilani and the men at the back of the van. "Can you let me go now?"

Garreth released my wrist. "Sorry. I only held on to you because you were hitting pretty hard." He dusted his knuckles over his cheek. "I'm pretty sure I'm going to be bruised tomorrow."

I scowled at him. "You'll still look pretty enough."

He lifted his brows as if assessing me with interest now, but I kept my scowl on my face. "You're not my type. I prefer men who don't kidnap me."

He winced. "I'm sorry about that, okay? Are you hurt?"

I did a mental calculation. Now that the adrenaline sliding in my veins had slowed, nothing actually hurt. There was a little throbbing in my head, but that was probably from the overflow of adrenaline. I hadn't technically been hurt.

I tested the handle of the door I was backed up against. It gave easily, and the door slid back. Jackson held up his hands as if he were under arrest. "Jesus, you can go anytime. I guess you really didn't get the invitation."

I shook my head. "I may have gotten it. I just didn't open it. I have a lot going on." No way was I going to explain to him that it looked like some piece of bullshit my ex-boyfriend would have sent me.

Garreth took a deep breath. "Okay, maybe we should start again. Hi, we're the Daylighters. We would very much like you to be part of the group. The photos you've taken so far have been amazing. And we can see why Xander is so taken with your work."

I frowned. "You've seen my work?"

"Well, when Xander considers new students, he picks the best of the best. And then he discusses his favorites with us, their strengths, their weaknesses. Then throughout the course of the year, when he gives critiques, we follow their progress. The photos of the kids in the market. That was really terrific."

I frowned. "You really do know my work."

Garreth nodded. "Yeah, they were great."

The warm flush of pride in my chest did something to stave off my irritation. "What does this group entail anyway?"

"We're headed to the studio near the Victoria and Albert Museum. From there, we confiscate your phone for the day, and we shoot in the city. Kind of gorilla stuff. A little more urban. A little grittier. It's just for the day and the night, and then you get to go home."

I slid my glance to Ilani, and she nodded her head. "Hey, I got my invitation, so I knew something like this was going to happen. I'm ready for it."

"I don't want to give up my phone though."

Garreth shook his head. "It's tradition. And if something is actually urgent, and someone calls you on it, we'll let you know."

"I need to text someone first."

Jackson shrugged. "Fine. Make it quick, then."

I glanced at my friends and the three idiots who thought it might be a good idea to kidnap me. The word *no* was on the tip of my tongue because their methodology was terrifying. But Ilani and Dane were there. And now that I could see their faces, I knew I wasn't just being kidnapped out of the park.

I nodded warily. "Listen, I'll come along. But if there's anything I don't like, I'm done."

Jackson nodded. "Fair enough. We already have our kits, so let's get going."

With another withering glare for Jackson, I texted Lex.

Abbie: *Will be shooting late. Rain check?*

I handed my phone to Jackson with a frown before settling back in the seat next to Ilani. I turned to her. "If we're being human trafficked, this is your fault."

She laughed. "If we are, I'm glad I'm with you. You'll put up a hell of a fight if we get in trouble."

Little did she know I'd spent much of my adult life being afraid.

Well, I was done being scared.

☙❧

ALEXI...

I checked my phone... for the twentieth time that afternoon.

No more texts from Abbie. Since the one saying she was shooting late, I hadn't heard from her.

You are officially pussy whipped.

That's, right. I had it bad. The worst thing was that I wasn't even trying to keep it a secret. I wanted to be with her, to spend as much time as possible with her. I was nuts.

Yeah, you're nuts. She doesn't know the truth.

There was a lot to talk about. And I was going to tell her. I didn't want to keep it from her. If this was the real thing, she had to know. All of it.

And she would understand. She had to. Because once I understood what I was feeling, I wasn't planning on letting her go. And I wasn't going to allow the whole situation with Gemma ruin everything either.

I'd had too many one-night stands and meaningless shag-buddy situations. Abbie was the first person I'd wanted to let in. I was itching to tell her everything, and I knew she wouldn't run.

You mean you hope *she won't.*

I typed in the code for the main entry door of her flat before taking the stairs two at a time.

Excited much? According to Xander, women liked it when blokes played it a little cool. But we were way past that point. I hoped to surprise her and make her dinner.

On her doorstep, I wiped my boots and shook off the rain, taking off my coat before I knocked on the door.

No one answered. I frowned and knocked again. Tension sat squarely between my shoulder blades. Had she forgotten we had a date tonight?

When she still didn't answer, I pulled out my phone and texted her again.

Alexi: *Your boyfriend is here to do naughty, debaucherous things to you. He's at the door. Open up.*

I waited, but the message didn't show as delivered. Was it possible she wasn't home? I heard footsteps and then smiled to myself. She'd probably let her phone die. I was going to buy her a million portable chargers.

When the door opened though, it wasn't Abbie. It was Faith. And she gave me a confused smile. "Uh, Lex? What are you doing here? Did plans change? Are we going out from here? I was just in the shower, but I don't think I got a text."

Shit. It seemed Abbie hadn't said anything about us to her friends yet, which suited me fine. I swallowed that dig against my conscience. It was handy that Faith and I weren't really that great of friends. She hadn't gone to Uni with me, so she didn't know about Gemma. And Faith was more Sophie's friend than in the core group with Max.

The lads, they knew about Gemma, so it was likely Sophie did too. But Faith didn't look like she wanted to cut off my balls so she probably didn't know. "Sorry. I was just looking for Abbie. We were going to... chat." *About what you twat?* "Uh, about a potential photography gig." That was plausible right?

Her short blond hair was visibly still damp and tousled. She must have been in the shower. "I just got back this morning from Ireland. She's not here. All she said was she was going to do some work tonight. So, I assume that meant you."

"Uh, yep. I haven't heard from her though, and I'm a little

worried." That was too much. Why would I be worried? I searched through my skull for a plausible reason for my concern.

But turned out I didn't need it. She was already thinking about where Abbie might be. "If she makes a plan, she sticks to it. She's anal about that. Like really compulsive. Like someone is gonna scream at her for going off book. So it's odd you haven't heard from her."

I pushed down the flare of anger. If I ever got my hands on that arsehole, I was going to kill him.

"I haven't spoken to her since early this morning."

Faith frowned then. "Come in. I'll try to locate her on Find my Friends."

I followed behind her, my worry dogging every step. "Any other friends you know of that might have an idea where she is?"

Faith shook her head. "I'm sure it's fine. She probably just got caught up with shooting, right? You know how she gets."

I nodded slowly, even as I pulled out my phone and texted my brother. "Yeah. Xander's the same way." *Then why doesn't it feel like she got caught up with shooting?* "It could be anything. I mean, if you're going to Sophie's, maybe she misinterpreted and went there?"

Faith shrugged. "Yeah, let me check with Sophie and see if that's where she headed."

She jogged into the back rooms and then came back with her phone. No, she isn't with Sophie, and Jasper offered that he hadn't seen her. Can't locate her on Find my Friends, either. It says 'location unknown,' so her phone is probably dead."

I ground my teeth then and groaned. "I'm seriously concerned something may have happened to her, Faith."

She fidgeted as she bit her nail. "It's not like her, to be honest. She doesn't just let her mobile die. And she's paranoid about safety. I'm a little concerned, too. It's not like her to completely vanish."

"Why do you say that?"

Faith shuffled on her feet. "Listen, it's not my place, but did she tell you anything about her past?"

The increased unease made the hairs on my arms stand up. "Yeah, about her ex?"

Faith nodded with what looked like a sigh of relief. "Oh good, she told you about Easton. Did she mention that he's been calling her?"

My brows snapped down. "What the fuck?"

"Yeah. You know, just calling and insisting she come home, demanding that she call him... but she hasn't been. She said that there was no way he would come to London or anything, but I mean, what if he did?"

Fuck. I hadn't received a message back from Xander, but Faith had a point. Based on Mom's and Jean Claude's connections, the family had a couple of detectives and inspectors we were on a first name basis with. "Looks like I'm calling in a favor."

CHAPTER TWO

ALEXI

I t turns out, it doesn't matter how rich you are. You can't buy a police investigation into someone who hasn't been missing at least twenty-four hours. The Detective Inspectors I'd called in favors with agreed to keep an eye out, but even their hands were tied.

Faith had stayed home in case Abbie showed up there, and Sophie was keeping an eye out at Max's. By the time I returned home to the barge for a quick shower and change of clothes, I was ready to rip out my hair. I needed to find her.

Was Faith right? Could Easton have taken her?

If the police weren't going to do anything, I still had other favors I could call in, and I'd use them all if that would get me to Abbie.

Ryan Buttersfield was an investigator I hired as a consultant when I wanted information on new companies and their owners. He did some work for the police as well, but mostly, he was the kind of guy that found people who didn't want to be found. He was also a kidnap and ransom specialist. He answered in one ring. "Mr. Chase? To what do I owe the honor?"

"Ryan, mate. Listen, I have a favor to ask."

"Is there any time you call me that isn't a favor?"

I shrugged. "I pay for my favors, don't I?"

"Yeah, but usually the things you have me looking at are a little tricky to get access to."

"I'm in a bind, mate. I need you." I wasn't above begging.

I knew this was dangerous territory. I felt myself spiraling out of control, but I didn't have time to focus on what that meant. Once she was home safe, I'd take a long look at my holiday to Crazytown.

His voice went deadly serious then. "What is it?"

"My girlfriend... she's missing."

There was a beat of silence. "What do you mean, *missing*?"

"Well, her phone is not on. The police won't look into it."

He was quick to ask, "Why won't the police look into it?"

I sighed. "She hasn't been missing that long. Just since this morning."

"Any reason you think she would be missing and not, you know, shopping or something?"

"She's not that kind of girl, and she has an ex. He used to hurt her."

The ice crept into Ryan's voice without any prodding at all. "Wanker. What's his name?"

I gave him the details I knew about Easton, thanks to Faith. "He's been calling her. Insistent on getting her back. It normally wouldn't be a big deal, but her phone is not on, and I'm just worried."

"Yeah, let me look into it. I'll at least see if I can locate the ex, and then we'll go from there."

"Thanks."

"And this one's free of charge."

I frowned. "You don't need to do that."

"Never told you about my sister, did I? The reason I look for things that can't be found?"

I shook my head even though he couldn't see me. "No."

"I'll tell you the whole sad story one day, but suffice it to say, she had a boyfriend like that. It didn't end well. So, I don't charge to give arseholes their due. Give me an hour."

"Thanks."

I ended the call with Ryan and started to pace. I still had a massive pile of work I needed to do for Toshino, but I couldn't focus. And even as I thought it through, it occurred to me that this might have nothing to do with Abbie's past, but rather my own.

He wouldn't do this, would he? It didn't matter whether I believed he would or not. The fact that Jean Claude sought to keep my and Xander's skills fresh by staging faux kidnappings meant he should have been my first call. But something like this was out of order. Even for him.

I was putting on my coat to head down to his office even as I rang him. He answered on the third ring. "Alexi, to what do I owe the honor? Usually, I'm calling you trying to set a meeting."

"If you fucking lay a hand on her, I will kill you."

There was a beat of silence. "Is there a reason you think I'd lay a hand on someone?"

"My girlfriend, she's gone."

Jean Claude's voice was firm. "I haven't laid a hand on Gemma. Why would I? She and her connections are basically the golden goose. She gives you legitimacy."

I frowned. "No, not Gemma. I'm talking about Abbie."

There was a beat of silence. "Might I remind you that the only girl anyone is aware of is Gemma? So, whoever this Abbie person is, I didn't touch her either."

"Don't be daft. I know you follow us."

"Look, yes, I may have men follow you, for your own protection, mind you, but if you have a dalliance, rest assured, she's not worth kidnapping. Not on my radar."

"I'm coming to see you. If I find her locked up in your fucking basement like the goddamn psycho you are, I swear to God, I will—"

Jean Claude's voice went icy. "You'll what? You'll kill me? Might I remind you, Your *Highness,* that you need to watch those words considering your past? And you're welcome to come here, but I haven't got anyone locked up in any basement. I was aware, yes, of your dalliance with the photographer. I'm also aware of your brother's obsession with her. But I haven't laid a hand on her."

I don't know why, but something told me to believe him. "Are you sure?"

He sighed, clearly exasperated. "No, I mistakenly kidnapped someone. It slipped my mind. We don't do this for fun and games, Alexi. We do this to keep you safe. Because when you finally sit on the throne, far be it from me to have you unprepared. That wasn't the oath I made to your grandfather."

I ran my hands through my hair, tugging as I went. "I swear to God, if you did something to her—"

"For all that is holy, Alexi. I wouldn't. Because she doesn't *matter* to me. The only thing that matters is your future. And Gemma, need I *remind* you, is your future. Not this African girl. Honestly, couldn't you at least find one more worthy? Or let Xander have this one? He'll never be your mother's successor."

That knot in my belly turned to an ugly, oily thing that threatened to drown me. "When I know she's safe, you and I are going to have a conversation about you saying bigoted things about her. Do you understand?"

"If you say so. She's not my concern. You are. You and Xander."

"Fuck."

"Might I suggest the police if she's gone missing?"

"They won't help. She hasn't been gone long enough."

Even Jean Claude seemed to agree with the police. "It's entirely possible, Your Highness, that she is merely busy or stuck on the tube, for the love of Christ."

"I have a bad feeling about this, Jean Claude."

"Alexi, may I speak freely?"

"So your previous bullshit was you holding back?" I snarked.

"Maybe this woman, this girl, really, perhaps she's not good for you, because I've never seen you act this way. You're acting desperate. Out of control. You're being reckless. If this woman can push you to this point, she can't possibly be good for you."

"I'll decide what's good for me." I hung up without waiting for a response.

I had one other avenue an ocean away. But calling in my Uncle Cassius would cause an international incident. My uncle might be king of a different nation, but he had power. And power moved the needle in my favor.

Is she worth setting off a proverbial nuke for? That answer was easy. Hell, yes.

My gut twisted into a knot. What the fuck was wrong with me?

Maybe everyone was right and she was fine. Maybe she'd simply left her phone somewhere, or she was in the tube with no signal.

Then why did I have a terrible feeling something was horribly wrong?

CHAPTER THREE

ABBIE

I was exhausted. But luckily, I hadn't been human trafficked, so yay. And despite my initial hesitation, the day and night with the Daylighters had been fantastic.

They'd known all the nooks and crannies of the city that I would never have been able to explore on my own. So it was kind of fun and all okay in the end.

But I was tired. And hungry. And I knew Faith was probably worried.

And Alexi. What was I going to tell Alexi? My phone was dead, and I needed to charge it before I could call him and explain. I hoped he hadn't been too worried.

When I put my key in the lock and shoved open the door, I found my living room full of people. Sophie, Max, Faith, Alexi, a couple of official-looking people, and Nick. I blinked rapidly. "I didn't know we were having a party."

The two official-looking men in suits cast glances at each other. One of them finally nodded his head in my direction. "Ms. Nartey, I assume?"

Christ. Just how much trouble was I in? I nodded slowly. "Yes."

"You're alive and well?" The other one asked.

I frowned. "Yes. Obviously." My gaze swung to Alexi's. "I hope this isn't for me."

I saw the muscle in his jaw tick. But his gaze swung over me repeatedly up and down, over and over, as if trying to catalogue my injuries or something.

"You're okay?" His voice was tight and more of a growl than actual words.

"Yeah. My phone died. I'm so sorry. There is an explanation for this. I hope all of you weren't too worried. The Daylighters sort of grabbed me. And—"

His brows furrowed. "Daylighters?"

I glanced around. "I'm not sure I'm supposed to say, but it's some photography secret society of Xander's former students. It's silly really, but we were just all over the city shooting during the day, and we did night shoots too." I swung my gaze to the official-looking men and assumed they were police. "I'm safe and sound."

The men in suits nodded at each other and put away their notepads. "Since Miss Nartey is back safe, it seems we're not needed."

Alexi nodded and thanked them. Faith showed them out.

Nick nodded at me. "It's good to see you Abbie. You gave us all a right scare."

I flushed. "I'm sorry. I didn't realize everyone would be so worried."

Alexi's voice was still tight. "Of course, we were worried. We care about you."

"Look, I didn't know they were going to take me, and they took my phone, and then it died and I couldn't call, and I didn't actually even have your number memorized to call on someone else's phone. There was nowhere to charge it and—"

He took my hand and squeezed it. "You're okay though?"

"I'm fine."

Faith strode back in and gave me a tight hug. "Well, I'm glad you're fine. Alexi was a little worried. And then he got me worried. And then I got Sophie worried."

Max and Sophie gave me hugs as well, and the two of them, along with Nick and Faith, made a hasty exit.

When it was just the two of us left, Alexi leaned against the fireplace and let go of my hand. "I was worried."

I shook my head. "You didn't need to be. I'm sorry I didn't call, but did you actually call the police?"

That muscle ticked in his jaw again. "Yeah, I did. I was up all night. We've called every friend you might have. I knew you didn't have class. I was worried that Easton had hurt you."

I flinched then forced myself to search his gaze. His normally soft silver eyes had gone hard and flint-like. "You thought Easton had me?"

"I did. I was scared for you."

"Okay. I get that. But the police? I mean, that was going a little overboard."

"Maybe, but I had to find you."

My heart started to flutter and not in a good way. Despite there only being the two of us in the room and the window being open to let in the early fall air, I couldn't breathe. My head started to pound, and the living room seemed to have shrunk.

Everything was too tight. Too constricting. I tried to take a step back, but my feet were frozen from the panic seizing me. "I'm not yours to worry about."

"Are you mad? I care about you, and you tell me you're not mine to worry about. After what we've already been through?"

I shook my head. "Alexi. I—" I swallowed hard. "I can't believe you called the police though."

"What was I supposed to do? You were gone. Faith didn't know where you were, and neither did Sophie. You have an abusive ex. He could have done something to you. And fuck, I don't know what I would have done if he had. I was already this close to breaking all the rules." He held up his thumb and forefinger. "I had someone investigate him."

I staggered back. "Alexi, this is... thank you for worrying about me. I've never had anyone this concerned about my well-being before, but I have to admit that it scares me a little."

He shut his eyes tight and took a deep breath, then another. And then one more. When his eyes opened, his gaze was softer, but I could tell he was still vibrating with anger. "I'm not mad at you, Abbie. I'm furious at him. I'm just furious. I don't know where to put all this tension and anger right now."

I took a deliberate step back and crossed my arms.

He frowned. "You think I would hurt you?"

I lifted my chin up. "No. But I don't do well with anger."

His hands gripped the edge of the sofa. "Abbie, I'm angry

because of the way I feel about you. I was going to break every rule I've ever had to find you. To make sure you were safe."

"I don't know what to do with that, Alexi. It terrifies me."

He frowned. "I'm not like him. I won't hurt you. How can you even compare me to him?"

I folded my arms. "He was possessive too."

Alexi ran his hands through is hair. "Okay. Fair enough. But all I want is your safety. I'm not trying to *own* you. Right now, what my heart is telling me is that you're mine to protect and that someone tried to hurt you. So, I'm having to calm myself down, bring it down several notches so that I don't hold on to this anger instead of holding you tight the way I want to."

The sweet sentiment wasn't lost on me. But I'd heard this kind of love before. Right before Eason would hurt me. He always couched the abuse as being because he loved me so much. I wasn't going to go through that again.

"Alexi, look. I'm sorry you were worried. But this? The police? It's too much. Too soon. It's stifling. And it scares me."

"Abbie, has anyone ever cared about you? Anyone ever worried about you? Worried about you not coming home? Worried about the bruises on your skin? Worried that something had happened to you?"

I bit my lip. A wash of embarrassment hit me hard. My voice was soft when I answered. "No."

"This is what it feels like when someone worries about you. I'm not being a possessive twat."

He was right. No one had ever worried about me before. Or cared that someone might hurt me. Not one person. No one in my family. "I know that's not your intention. But it feels like that."

"You're going to compare me to him? He *hurt* you."

"I'm sorry. I can't help it." My voice was small.

He nodded. "I've never felt like this about anyone before. And I don't know what to do with it."

Though his words gripped my heart and stuck their hooks in, they wrapped around it and claimed it in a way that I didn't want it claimed, in a way that I was afraid of what it meant. "You're turning me inside out, Alexi. I want to go slow, but how I feel about you, it scares me."

"Abbie, I would *never* do anything to hurt you. And I recognize that you need time to understand that."

I wanted nothing more than to believe him, to let myself freefall into those feelings. But I couldn't. "I do. Maybe we need to put the brakes on things for a minute."

His brows furrowed. "What?"

I could feel the fissures in my heart forming. But the fear won out. "I'm sorry."

His gaze searched mine for a long moment, and I braced myself, waiting for the anger to spill over. I waited for him to turn into a man I didn't know. But nothing happened. Instead, he merely nodded. "Fair enough. You know where to find me when you realize I'm not him."

The soft click of the door as he walked out was somehow more devastating than if he'd slammed it.

I should have felt relief. I should have felt safe. Instead. I just felt hollow.

ALEXI...

I hadn't slept all fucking night.

Abbie's words were in a constant loop in my head. Too much too soon. She'd equated how the hell I felt about her to her bleeding ex.

I'd been worried about her, and she'd compared me to that psychopath. Ryan had come back with all kinds of information about her ex.

Oh, right. And you semi-stalking her isn't a reason for her to be worried.

That piece of logic didn't sit well, so I was going to leave it alone for a bit. For now, I was going to deal with my brother and his fucking Daylighters.

Stalker much?

After this, I was done until she decided she was ready. It might physically kill me, but I could do it. She was gun shy, which was more than understandable. But I knew I wanted her, and I could feel that this was real.

She felt it too. I could tell. Hell, she'd as much as said so herself. She just needed some time to get over her fear. I didn't really have much choice but to be patient. In the meantime, Xander and I needed to have a fucking conversation.

Unfortunately, at dinner I wouldn't be able to throttle him like I wanted to. But there might be time for that later.

When he finally showed up at the restaurant twenty minutes late, he threw his hands up. "Mate, I'm sorry. I was shooting, and you know how it is."

I scowled at him. "So, you're just going to show up late, not even wondering why I've been trying to reach you all damn day."

I'd picked a Puerto Rican restaurant just off Kensington High Street. It was small and tucked away. I knew the owner, and they served some killer Mofongo. So at least I'd be full and happy before I killed my brother.

He scowled as he signaled to the bartender. "What the fuck is wrong with you? Who took a piss in your Weetabix?"

"You don't know what the fuck could be wrong with me?"

He shook his head. "No. Why are you in such a stroppy mood?"

Like he had no fucking clue. "I'm in a stroppy mood because some of your little disciples kidnapped my girlfriend."

His brows snapped down. "What the fuck are you on about?"

My gaze searched his face. "You really don't know."

Xander shook his head. "I don't know what the hell you are talking about. Is Abbie okay?"

I frowned at him. His shoulders were tense. His brows were furrowed, and his lips were pressed into a thin line. He was angry.

He hadn't known. But his tension brought up a whole other point of concern. He wanted her. He wanted what was mine. I already knew it, but to see it on his face like that made me bristle. He couldn't have her. I didn't care what I had to do. She was mine, and she was staying that way.

Have you told her that yet? So much for patience.

"You don't know about your Daylighters, or whatever the fuck they call themselves?"

"What about the fucking Daylighters?"

I sat back and crossed my arms. "Well, apparently, they

grabbed her off the street and practically forced her to join their little club."

His ears went red first. I knew for a fact that was his first anger response before the fists started to fly. "They fucking did what?"

"They nicked her off the street, in broad daylight."

"I'm going to fucking kill them."

"Aren't they your group?"

"They're my fucking former students and teaching assistants, but I don't control them."

"I spent nearly twenty-four hours worried something had happened to her. Called the police and everything."

Xander blew a long whistle. "Fuck."

"And all along, your people had her."

"What the fuck are you talking about Lex? They're not *my people*. They're students. They have this secret society. It has nothing to do with me."

"I spent the whole fucking night looking for her, worried something had happened. I almost called Uncle Cassius."

His eyes went wide. "You almost called our uncle for help? The bloody King of the Winston Isles an ocean away. Why didn't you call me?"

And therein lay the rub. I'd called the police. I'd called Jean Claude. I'd had Faith on speed dial. I'd almost pulled in my family. But I hadn't called the only person I knew would be as concerned as I was. Jealousy was a jealous mad bitch with an attitude. "I texted you when I couldn't find her."

His brow furrowed deeper. "My student vanishes, and it doesn't occur to you to *call* me?"

I frowned. "No. She's my responsibility."

His brows rose then. "Does she know that?"

"She does now."

Xander scowled at me. "She's not good for you. Look at you, the way you're acting around her."

The sting of his words echoed both Jean Claude's and Abbie's, that all of this was too much. "What? And you think you'd be better for her?"

He didn't really have any recourse. He knew he was bad for her. "Whether I'm good for her or not isn't the point. You called the fucking police? You were about to have the whole London underground network searching for her, putting her on their radar? I don't like what she's doing to you, Lex."

I shook my head. "I might have overreacted."

Xander laughed and sat back. "You think so?"

"I was worried. You don't know why." I wondered just how close they were.

"Go on then. Tell me why."

I shook my head. "If she wanted you to know, she would have told you. In the meantime, I'm going to need you to back off. No more flirting with her."

He laughed. "If she flirts with me, what am I supposed to do?"

I ground my teeth. "She won't. I'm not going to fight you over a woman, Xan. Especially not this one. She's mine."

"What, you think you can just declare that and make it true?"

I sighed and forced the tension to leave my shoulders as I rolled them back. "I love you. You're my brother. The shit we've been through together, the plans we've made together... You're the most important person in the world to me. Nothing is getting in the way of that, but I can't let her go."

I watched the muscle in Xander's jaw tick. "Can't or won't, Lex?"

"Right now, it feels an awful lot like can't."

He nodded slowly as he warily watched me. "You're serious about this girl?"

I swallowed hard. "Yeah, I am."

And then he poked at the one soft spot that he knew I wouldn't refute. "Fair enough. I'll back off. I'm not the kind of guy who deserves that kind of love, anyway."

I winced. "Fuck, Xan, that's not what I meant."

He waved me off. "Look, I get it. You saw her first. But you need to tell her about Gemma, and you need to do it quickly. Because if you hurt her, as much as I love you, I will hurt you."

My gaze met his eyes, and they were a mirror of my own, the same silvery slate gray framed by thick, dark lashes. And he was deadly serious. I nodded my agreement. "I will tell her. I have to. I'm not used to feeling this way about anyone."

His eyes softened then. "It couldn't have happened to a better bloke."

I could see that he meant it. "Xan, you deserve love too, you know."

He shrugged. "Yeah, yeah. None of that is important now. You're not the only one who's been bitten by the bug. I see how she looks at you."

I wanted to say something. Anything to make him feel better. Except I couldn't give her up. She was *mine*. That word sounded awful, even to me. Fuck, maybe she was right.

Maybe I *was* too much like her ex. But fuck, the idea of letting her go made me sick to my stomach.

"I'm telling her."

"You better. How do you think Gemma is going to take it?"

I shrugged. "Well, Gemma's more of a habit than anything else. She's one of my best friends, so I want to protect her. But I need to finally think about myself, and I hope Gemma will understand that."

"Abbie's going to ask questions, you know that. And not just about Gemma. It's the kind of person she is."

I nodded slowly. "If she asks about the past, I'll tell her."

Xander's brows lifted. "You really do care about her."

I rubbed at my chest. "She was gone for fucking twenty-four hours, and this part right here in my chest... It felt like I'd been pierced by something that didn't tickle. Not knowing where she was, or what was wrong with her, or who might have her... I fucking lost it, Xan."

He whistled low. "Jesus fucking Christ, you really are in love with her."

I frowned at that. "All I know is that I've never felt like this before. I'll take some suggestions on how to make it stop."

He laughed then. "I'm not sure you can, little brother. Love. It couldn't have happened to a nicer bloke." He raised his glass of wine. "I'm not thrilled, mind you. This version of you scares me. Be careful, because she triggered something in you that you might not be ready for."

I nodded slowly. "I feel protective of her."

Xander watched me, his eyes narrowing. "I know. It's the

same way you feel about me. And you and I both know how dangerous that is."

When we left the restaurant, Xander inclined his head across the street. "You got a ride? I brought the Bugatti today."

I rolled my eyes. "How do you have any money left in your trust fund if you're spending it all on supercars?"

Xander laughed. "You know full well I don't touch that thing. It pays to be a famous artist. People will put any price on art. It's ridiculous. All because it makes them feel something."

"And you're willing to cash in on that, aren't you?"

He grinned. "Hey, it's an honest way to earn a living. It also means that I don't have to touch Dad's money."

"That, I completely understand. No worries though. I brought my car."

He shook his head. "Still driving that BMW?"

"What do you mean 'still'? That car is brand new."

"God, when are you going to learn? We're Chases. We need a bit of flash."

"*You* need a bit of flash. I'm resigned to be the second son. I don't need to be flashy. I can be understated and still be the sexier brother."

Xander's laugh was full of mirth. "Yeah. I see you're still the delusional brother too. We both know I'm sexier."

"You wish."

Suddenly, Xander whipped around over his shoulder, and his body tensed.

His awareness put me on alert. And then I could feel it too. A prickle. Like a sixth sense that something was off. I whipped around too. Xander asked, "Do you feel that, Lex?"

"Yeah, like someone's watching?"

He nodded. "You think it's Jean Claude?"

I shrugged. "Fuck if I know. I gave him an earful when I thought he'd taken Abbie."

Xander frowned. "You thought *he* took Abbie?"

"With him anything is possible."

"Jesus you really do have it bad." He laughed then. "Better you than me. After all, what would all the single ladies in London do with me off the market?"

He was joking, but I could tell he was still tense. "Just in case Jean Claude is holding a grudge, why don't you give me a ride to my car."

"Good plan. We always do better when we stick together, little brother."

Wasn't that the truth. I just hoped Abbie wouldn't come between us.

CHAPTER FOUR

ABBIE

Anywhere but here.
I would have paid cash money to be anywhere else but class. A Russian Gulag, running the New York City Marathon in the dead of winter. Anywhere else.

But no.

My stomach was already churning over the fight with Alexi. And then Faith and Sophie had given me the third degree about him wanting to know what the hell was going on. I'm pretty sure they didn't believe my 'we've become friends' lie by omission. And then, well, I'd seen the photos I'd taken with the Daylighters.

They were, in a word... bad. Since we'd skipped critique last week due to Xander having a show, I'd had to pick the best of the lot between the garden party and what I'd taken with the Daylighters. And there wasn't an inspiring image amongst them. Not one.

So I knew what was coming. I'd lost sleep over what was

coming. I was poised and ready to pack my bags over what was coming.

I hadn't had the good sense to get my pain over with early this time, so instead, I was last for critique. When Xander pulled up my images, I slunk down into my seat. I knew they weren't great. I knew they were only pretty pictures with no depth. I'd managed to find one or two from the previous assignment that I'd dropped in there, but as a whole, the images were from that god-awful garden party. There was one of Lex thrown in that I'd taken in St. Albans. He'd been reaching out his hand to me before entering a church.

That photo was cheating though. That wasn't love in his eyes, but it was a great photo, the only great one in the bunch. I knew the rest were abysmal. I didn't need anyone else to tell me they were.

Ilani, bless her, leaned over in her chair. "They're not so bad. Really."

But I knew she was just saying it to be nice.

When Xander spoke, I wished I could just run and hide. He met my gaze directly, and I couldn't read anything in his stare.

"I'm going to open up the floor for your thoughts on Abbie's photos this week."

Shit. My friends were going to rip me a new one. No matter that I took care with their feelings for each of their critiques. They had no loyalty to me. They only cared about scoring points with Xander.

One person said, "Flat."

Another called out, "Boring."

One even asked, "Did Abbie do these? Last week's were so good. These are just..." His voice trailed off.

Ilani tried to come to my defense. "C'mon guys. They're not *that* bad. Maybe a little trite. They just need a little oomph. I mean there are those with the kid krumpers and the one with the hot guy at the end. That one captured the essence of the assignment."

Xander glared at Ilani, and she immediately shut up, sliding me an apologetic glance. And so it went for the next ten minutes. For my part, I took it like a woman. Chin up, back straight. Well, as much as I could straighten my back while trying to crawl under my desk and hide.

At the end of class, I'd never been so relieved in my life. Ilani handed me my scarf. "C'mon. Let's go get you a drink. I think you could use it."

"Not so fast, Miss Bruce. I need to speak to Miss Nartey for a moment."

Xander's voice was neutral, but still my heart hammered against my ribs. This couldn't be good. Would he kick me out of the program? Hell, it wasn't like I'd had the worst review in the class. Roger's critique had been far more scathing.

I slunk up to the table at the center of the small auditorium. "Yes, Xander?"

He folded his arms across his chest. "Do you want to tell me what's going on?"

I swallowed. "I—I'm not sure–"

He interrupted. "Abbie, your work is better than this. Even your portfolio you sent for admission was better than most of these. I know you're capable of more, so why are you aiming for mediocrity?"

I rubbed my forehead. What the hell was I supposed to say? I certainly wasn't going to make excuses for myself. "They're not my best. I know I can do better."

"Whatever's distracting you, get rid of it. Even if it's my brother. It's compromising your work. I would hate to waste my time with you all term and have you not turn out how I expect. No more distractions."

Damn. How the hell could this be my life? I wasn't the one who got scolded by the teacher. I'd always prided myself on doing better than expected. Exceeding expectations was my special talent. And I'd failed. All because I'd been too caught up in Lex to do my assignment properly.

"I won't let you down again."

"You have a promising career. I'd hate to see that thwarted."

I nodded stiffly. "I understand."

"You're a better artist than this, Little Bird. I want to see your best from now on."

I shifted on my feet. "You will. Just, don't send me home. I can do better."

His brow furrowed. "Is that what you think?"

"Well it did cross my mind."

He watched me more closely but said nothing to dispel my concern. Finally, he said, "You're all right though? After your... ordeal?"

I flushed. "You heard about that?" I rushed to add. "Please tell the guys I'm sorry for roughing them up. I just thought I was being snatched off the street, so I fought back."

His brows lifted. "They pulled you off the street?"

I blinked. The surprise on his face was genuine. Which

meant he hadn't heard about it from the other Daylighters. So that left one person who could have told him. Alexi. "Uhm, it's not as bad as it sounds." I tried again because that did sound pretty bad. "It worked out in the end."

"Rest assured, I'll be having a word with them." His voice was icy and set a terrified shiver through me.

"I—I don't want anyone to get in trouble, and it turned out fine. I swear. I was probably—"

He cut me off. "Miss Nartey, did you consent to being dragged off the street?"

"No. Not exactly but—"

His gaze narrowed. "Did you consent to being frightened?"

"No. But I didn't open the invit—"

"If you're about to give me some bollocks about how you eventually consented to join them, save it. The way they went about it was all wrong. Are we in agreement?"

Well, he did have a point. "Yes. It's just that they didn't mean—"

His slate eyes went glacial. "I think it's probably best you don't make excuses for people who hurt you or put you in harm's way."

Direct. Fucking. Hit.

Shame slammed into me. It didn't matter that he had no idea just how close to home he'd hit. I still felt the emotional blow. "Understood. May I go?"

He gave me a terse nod, and I forced my feet to move. I trudged out of the auditorium to find Ilani waiting for me.

"Well, how did it go?"

I shook my head. "I'm far too sober to be able to talk about it yet." I would have to make some changes if I wanted to survive another critique.

⚜

ABBIE

I hadn't really had the time to call home, but after the last few days, I needed something familiar. Something to steady me.

Faith called for me from down the hall. "Abbie, get a move on. Max will be here to pick us up any minute."

"I'll be right there, Faith. I just need to make a quick call." Calling home shouldn't make me feel slightly nauseated, but it did. Though it wasn't like I was calling my mother, who would in all likelihood tell me to call Easton.

"Hello?" The moment, I heard my father's lilting accent, a sense of calm washed over me. He'd always had that effect on me. He had a way of keeping me focused.

"Hi, Daddy." It was hard to keep my voice from wavering, but I put in a good effort.

"Abena, is something wrong?"

"No. I uhm, haven't talked to you in a while, and I just wanted to hear your voice."

There was a beat of silence. Maybe I'd made a mistake? Maybe I should have called my sister Ama instead for the boost of reassurance.

"Well, now you hear it. Is everything well?"

I wanted to laugh at our stilted conversation as I remembered why I usually spoke to my mother. "Yes, fine. Just, uhm, fine."

He cleared his throat. "You never were good at masking your emotions. You might as well just tell me."

"I'm afraid you'll just tell me to come home."

Another beat of silence. "Abena, you're an adult. I can't make you do anything you don't want to do. You made the decision to go, so you must want this enough to be there. What's troubling you?"

Exhausted, I exhaled and slumped my shoulders as I sank onto my bed. "I just, I had a bad critique, and it's messing with me a little. I'm starting to wonder if you were right, if I should have gone to law school instead. My professor is pissed. And I feel, I don't know... lost, I guess."

One of the things I always appreciated most about my father was that he took his time to choose his words.

"Are you giving your all?"

"Of course I am, Dad." Except I could have worked harder on the last assignment if I hadn't been distracted by Lex drama.

"Are you sure?"

I already regretted this call. "I get it, Dad. I should be working harder. I understand." *Next time you're wishing for a slice of home, Abbie, just don't.* I shouldn't have called.

He sighed. "No. You misunderstand. Abena, you've always been the one who worried most about what your mother and I think. You've always been the most cautious. But when you see something you want you go after it. I have always admired your tenacity, but I don't hear it in your voice now."

He admired something about me? "I've never had a professor tell me they're disappointed before. I'm used to being confident, at least about this. I might be a mess everywhere else, but this... I'm supposed to know how to do this. And now I feel like I'm on loose footing. It scares me."

"It should scare you." He dropped his voice for emphasis. "But it should also invigorate you. You're a Nartey. You fight. Do what challenges you. Don't settle on doing what will get you the easy remarks from your professor. Do the things that are difficult for you."

Tears pricked my eyes, and I rapidly blinked them away. He was right. Xander was right. I'd played it safe with the pictures from the party. I'd taken the easy way out. My focus had been somewhere else. *On Alexi.* Maybe I'd been too focused on him. I'd sworn I wasn't going to lose myself in another guy, and already that was happening, like it had with Easton. The party had been a prime place to work on portraits like Xander said, and I'd blown it.

"I—I really don't want to disappoint anyone. Least of all myself."

His voice gentled. "The only way you can do that is to not push yourself. In all areas of your life."

All areas. Was he talking about Easton? "Dad, I'm sorry to put you in the middle, but could you tell mom not to tell Easton what I'm up to anymore? It doesn't help."

"I can do that." His voice went deeper, gruffer. "I'm glad you're out there on your own. It's a chance to get a different perspective and maybe meet some new people. People who will nourish you." He was silent for a moment before he added, "I will make sure Easton and your mother do a better job of respecting your space."

My heart caught in my throat. Did he know about

Easton? *No. He couldn't.* But maybe he'd known I was unhappy all that time. "I— Thanks, Daddy. I needed to hear that."

"Good. Now send me a picture. One of your good ones. I have some empty wall space in my office."

I laughed. "Could you be more specific? I have lots of good ones."

"See, Abena? You sound better already."

After hanging up with my father, I picked up the book Xander had given me and thumbed through it. The portraits were exquisite. Haunting, even. They were unlike anything I'd ever done before. But maybe it was time to try. I'd taken several of Alexi last weekend. Some of them might even work.

Warmth spread through me, just thinking about him. But I had to watch myself. Already my split focus had put me on shaky ground. If I wanted that position, it would mean spending more time with my camera and less in Alexi's arms. The only problem was that I didn't think I could stay away from him.

ABBIE...

"So how are things with you and the young man?"

I shifted uncomfortably on my seat. *Way to just go in for the pain, Doc.* "Um, Alexi is fine. I guess."

Dr. Kaufman slid her glasses to the tip of her nose, making her look somehow older and wiser than she probably was. "Don't deflect. What's going on?"

I rolled my shoulders. "Ah, he's... God, I don't even know how to explain him."

"Are you following the same patterns?"

I frowned. "I feel like I am."

"Explain."

"The thing is he's different. He's the kind of boyfriend most people would want. He's attentive, and sweet, and fun, and he listens. He *really* listens."

Dr. Kaufman sat back and pushed her glasses back up her nose. "So, what's the problem?"

"The problem is he's rich and entitled. And he's possessive. *So* possessive."

She lifted a brow.

"There's a part of him that's just so sure we're *supposed* to be together. The other day, there was this prank. This photography group grabbed me, and we spent the day and the biggest part of the night taking pictures. I texted that I'd be late, and he called the police."

She frowned. "Because you were late?"

Heat crept up my neck. "Well, I—" I took a deep breath. "I was gone for a day and a night. He freaked out because I'd told him about my history with Easton."

"So you were gone for a day and a night, and he didn't know where you were, and then he called the police. I assume other steps were taken?"

I swallowed. "Yes. He tried to find me, as did my flatmate. But then he overreacted."

"You think he overreacted?"

"What was I supposed to do? I couldn't call because my phone was dead. The next thing I know, he's mobilized my roommate, my friends, and the police. He was out for blood, ready to kill anyone who might have hurt me."

Dr. Kaufman nodded slowly. "And this possessiveness you speak about, is this how Easton would act?"

I frowned at that. "Easton was different. It was more about him *having* to know where I was. He certainly would never call the police. But he would've called my friends, but not because he was worried, but more because he was angry."

"And this young man, Alexi, was he angry?"

I nodded. "He was furious. But not *at* me." I felt the need to explain him somehow. Even though his anger scared me. "He was furious at the group that took me in the first place, and that they scared me, that he didn't know where I was. I think he was scared *for* me."

Dr. Kaufman nodded. "Do you see the similarities in their responses?"

I nodded. "Of course. And it frightens me."

"And how are they different?"

"Look, I know that they're different. They're different men with different intentions. But I can't help my reaction. I walked into my flat and the police were there, and his best friend, my best friend, and everybody was standing around worried, and I didn't like it."

"What didn't you like about it?"

"I felt like I wasn't free. That I wasn't my own person."

"Okay. Did you feel like you were in danger? Did you feel like he was trying to control where you went?"

"I—" I considered this. I thought it through. "No, I don't think he was trying to control where I went. But he completely overreacted. And I don't want to be controlled. I don't like it."

"That's good that you know what you don't like. That's one of the key things. But why do you equate what he did to what Easton would have done?"

"He was so mad. I just kept waiting for him to lash out, to be angry."

"Did he put his hands on you?"

I shook my head. "No."

"Did he express anger toward you?"

I frowned. "No, but he *was* angry."

"Okay, what was he angry at?"

I ran my hand through my braids. "He was worried. Scared. It's just that kind of intensity... I don't understand it, and it scares me. I don't want to get caught up in the same kind of Easton thing."

She inhaled a deep breath and then sat forward. She studied me very closely before pulling her glasses off. "Abena, while I do have some reservations about the level of intensity between you and this young man, I want you to start getting to a place where you realize their actions are *different*. As are their motivations. What would have happened with Easton if you'd walked in after twenty-four hours of no call and no contact?"

I swallowed hard. "He would have been furious. I would've been bloody for weeks. I was scared to ever let my phone die."

"Right. You learned to never let your phone die. And with this young man, while unintentional, your phone did die. What happened?"

I shrugged. "He overreacted and called the police."

"Yes, and what else?"

I swallowed. "Nothing."

She raised a brow.

I pursed my lips. Why couldn't I just hide? I hated therapy. *No you don't.* "Okay, I pushed him away and told him it was too much and we needed to put on the brakes."

"Yes." She twirled her pen. "What were you feeling when you saw that Alexi had mobilized everyone to find you?"

I sighed. "I felt safe. Wanted. Taken care of."

"And you don't trust it?"

I shook my head. In for a penny in for a pound. "No, not really."

"Has he ever given you any indication that you can't trust him?"

I shook my head. "No. But Easton was like that in the beginning."

Her patience with me alone was worth every penny. "I want you to think about that over the next couple of weeks until I see you again. I want you to really examine that. With Easton, were there any red flags? Things that you saw but dismissed. Things that you ignored, things that you would rewind the clock and go back to."

I nodded. "I mean, I guess there were. I just— I don't want to get caught in that position again."

"I agree. I don't think you should get caught in that position. I encourage you to date this young man because I think you need to experience life. I think it's good for you. I also think it's good for you to set boundaries about what you're looking for and what you're *not* looking for."

"I was clear. I don't want anyone that rich, or titled, or possessive. And I've got that guy. And how did I end up here?"

She shrugged. "Of all those things, what is the actual problem?"

I didn't like this part of therapy. This forcing myself to open up and glare down at things that scared me. I wasn't a fan. "I don't like the possessiveness. That's what scared me the most."

"Okay, have you had a conversation about that?"

"No."

"Don't you think maybe you should?"

I shook my head. "I don't want to hurt him."

"Right. You don't want to hurt him, but what about you? Maybe you don't want to set the boundaries for yourself?"

"I don't know. I don't even know how to begin having that conversation without fear."

"Okay, that's understandable. But does it do you any good to hide how you feel?"

"Ah, I mean, I guess I could."

"What would be the worst thing that could happen if you said, I don't like the possessiveness, and it concerns me."

"It could end up like Easton. I could be trapped."

"Or?"

I swallowed hard. "I could hurt him, and he could leave me."

She nodded. "Right. So, that is your real fear?"

"Oh my God, what is wrong with me?"

Her smile was soft and warm. "Honestly, nothing that hasn't been wrong with women for centuries. We want some things that we're afraid to ask for. If you care about this young man, have a conversation with him. If you are legitimately afraid of him, have a friend be there, or tell him you can't see him anymore. But if you are afraid of your past, this is the only way forward... before it costs you your future."

"I'm scared."

"That's good. It's good to say that. To experience the emotion. You let yourself feel that. Are you scared of him or scared of your feelings?"

"I'm scared of my feelings. I don't want to feel like this. I've been burned."

"Haven't we all? Now granted, you have been burned more severely than most. Just see what happens when you talk to him. You don't know him until you see his response. And then we'll move on from there. Because what's the worst that could happen? You ask him for what you want. Do you get it?"

She had a point. My whole life, I'd always been afraid to ask for what I wanted. Terrified. There were ramifications. It meant I'd be unloved. Because when I did ask for what I wanted, my family shunned me, my boyfriend hit me, and my life crumbled. And so now, to ask for a little bit of breathing room, while also having the man, that scared me. And I had no idea how to go about doing that.

"Can I ask him to do something easier?"

She chuckled softly. "No. Because you're trying to grow. You're trying to be the best version of you. And one of those things is being able to ask for what you want. Now, I'm not going to say you're going to ask for these things without fear. There's always an element of that. But remember that courage is not being afraid; it's being afraid of managing that, right?"

I crossed my arms. "I'm not sure I like you."

She laughed. "You know, you are not the first patient to tell me that."

CHAPTER FIVE

ABBIE

I was nervous.

I'd known I was making a mistake when I pushed Alexi away, but to have Dr. Kaufman reiterate that to me made me angry and ashamed.

I had a perfectly good man in front of me. One who had turned over every stone to find me and keep me safe instead of turning every stone over so he could hurt me. And I'd rejected him.

Like an idiot.

So I was going to say sorry. When I texted Sophie to ask her what one wears for a *mea culpa*, her response was to be expected. *Stilettos, trench coat, nothing else.*

Even I wasn't that badass. Besides, what if he was angry enough with me to not speak to me, which he was within his rights too. Then I'd be stuck in the middle of London... in no panties and a trench coat.

After a night and a full day of thinking through what Dr.

Kaufman said, I really had to confront the fact that he was different from Easton.

That I felt different when I was with him. And while the force of the pull between us terrified the hell out of me, his actions were about concern not about control. And I needed to find a way to trust myself and my ability to communicate with him when I felt like I was being stifled.

Just because he had a strong personality didn't mean he was a controlling asshole. Possessive, maybe. Controlling, no.

I did opt for stilettos, but I couldn't very well wear nothing, so I chose a slinky red dress instead. The kind of thing I was getting used to wearing now.

When I stepped onto the barge, I had to steady myself for the gentle rocking. This was something out of French movies. Barges on the Seine that were beautifully decorated and well appointed. Replace the Seine with the Thames, and this glorified houseboat was incredible. Just how rich was he?

There were a few other barges docked at Oyster Pier. Sophie had said technically this area was the Left Bank. Faith had said Battersea. Either way, as I walked up, I knew I was in for something wholly different.

With a deep breath, I sucked it up. Because if you couldn't wear big girl panties and apologize, then what was the point? At the top of the plank, I knocked, praying that he would be home. I'd seen his car in the parking lot, so I knew that he was at least in the vicinity. But what if he'd gone for a run? Or was at a friend's place? Or what if he was at Xander's? Or what if he had a girl over?

Just because you had a fight, it doesn't mean he's got a girl over.

Just because Easton would tell me that I was replaceable all the time, it didn't mean that Alexi felt the same way. It looked like I had a lot of baggage to unpack in this whole relationship thing.

Finally, I heard footsteps, and a cold sweat broke out on my skin. Oh God, was it too late to run away? How far could I really get in my stilettos?

I looked down at my heels and realized I wouldn't get very far in these shoes. When Alexi tugged the door open, he was wet and in a towel.

Holy hell. I swallowed hard. "Oh, uh, hi. I— I'm sorry. I guess I should have called."

His brows lifted. "Abbie, I didn't expect to see you."

"If you're busy, I'll just go—" Because when in doubt, run.

He shook his head. "I'm not busy. I was just in the shower, clearly."

My gaze rolled over his broad shoulders and then flickered over his chiseled chest with the Gemini tattoo and the dusting of hair that led to very well-defined abs and an intriguing happy trail.

Focus.

I snapped my gaze up to his to find a smirk on that pretty mouth, then he lifted a brow and said, "Ah, right. Okay. Come in."

I nodded slowly. "Right, sure." So far, I was really winning at the convo starters.

"Is everything okay?" The concern crept into his voice, and I was quick to assure him.

"Yeah, I'm fine. I just, um, I just wanted to talk to you."

"Why don't I go throw some clothes on?"

My disappointment was palpable. "No, you don't have to do that on my account."

This time he grinned. "You want to have this conversation with me in a towel?"

My gaze flicked over him again, and I nodded even as I said, "No."

He crossed his arms then, and the motion made his biceps bulge. "So, which is it? Do you want me to put clothes on or don't you?"

"Um, yyy... no. Yes. Yes. Yes, of course. You be as comfortable as you want to be. It's your house. Er, barge. Whatever."

Still chuckling to himself, he headed to the right into what was probably the bedroom area. "I'll be right back."

Once he was gone, I let myself fully freak out about my surroundings. For starters, his living room, dining room, and kitchen area were an open-concept design, modern enough to make most HGTV enthusiasts proud.

The area was huge. Inside, it was nearly as big as my parents' house. Hardwood floors met steel and glass and gorgeous white granite in the kitchen, with what looked like oak paneling around the island.

Brass fixtures hung as pendant lights both over the island and the smaller dining area.

While the color palette was mostly white and grey, he'd warmed up the space by adding some of Xander's work to the walls and plush, soft looking fabrics in the living room throws and pillows.

I couldn't help but nose around the barge. On the bookshelves, there were a few knick-knacks, but mostly there were photos. Xander's prints were nearly as recognizable to me as my own work. Even though I'd never seen these, there was something about the style. There were also a couple of framed photos on the shelves. Him and Xander. Him, Nick, and Gemma. His mother. But mostly, there were books. Yes, there was the obvious smattering of business books but also Hemingway and Austen. The Austen confused me. But there was also Orwell and Bradbury.

"I see you found the books."

I nodded slowly. "I like it. Some of my favorites are shelved here."

He'd changed into jeans and a snug-fitting henley that did nothing to hide his ridiculous body. "My mother has a thing about books. They're her escape. She has passed on that love to me and Xander, I guess."

I turned and nodded. "Sorry. I didn't mean to snoop."

He shook his head. "I mean, they wouldn't be on display if I didn't want you to look. Besides, I figured you would have already had your opportunity to snoop if I'd had you by the other night."

Ouch. Direct hit.

"Right. Um, so I just—" Now that I was here in front of him, I didn't know what to say or how to act. It all felt new and confusing and awkward as hell.

"Would you like some tea? A drink?"

I shook my head. "Um, no thanks. I—" He stood perfectly still, patient, watching me. I could still feel the tension vibrating between us. "Okay, I'm sorry. I don't know how to do this. But I want to apologize."

His brow lifted. "For what?"

"I shouldn't have been angry with you. You were worried about me, and I get that."

He nodded slowly. "I *was* worried about you."

"I just walked in and there were all those people, and I freaked. And it's not your fault. It's me and the caravan of baggage I have behind me. I know you're not him. I know you were acting out of concern, and you weren't looking to control me. It's just in the moment, I started to feel claustrophobic and panicked." I shrugged. "It felt eerily similar to many other times when I wasn't exactly where I was supposed to be and Easton would rally the troops. And it would look like concern, but after... There would be pain."

He inhaled deeply then let the air out slowly. "I would never hurt you. I want to give you the assurance you need about that, but I don't know how. I'm not him, Abbie. We have completely different motivations."

"I know. I'm just now becoming aware of it really, I guess. Everything from my past colors every decision I make, everything I do, and you and I—it's inexplicable. And it is terrifying because I *want* to be around you all the time, and it was intense, and—" I shook my head. "I can't even describe it. When I'm near you, it just feels like I'm *supposed* to be there, and that scares me too because I have lost myself before in one relationship, and I know that this is a very different scenario."

"It is."

"Logically, I know that. And it feels different. But I don't know what to do with the intensity between us. So it was easier to push you away instead of examining all the feelings individually."

"Look, I know I overreacted. I was just concerned. But I'm not going to pretend that I wouldn't do it all over again the exact same way. You don't believe me yet, but I really care about you. And if you're hurt or need something, I will be right there. And I'll work as long as it takes to try to convince you of that."

I nodded. "I met with Dr. Kaufman, and she had me really look at my motivation and how I needed to own the place I've come from and not from the place of the embarrassment of everyone knowing my business. I need to look at it as something that could give me strength to not make the same choices."

He stood with his arms crossed, studying me intently. I could feel his anger, but he kept it banked. "I could kill him for making you afraid."

The anger scared me, but I also saw now that it wasn't directed at me... and it wouldn't be. Slowly I forced the words out to explain why his concern worried me.

"I once went with my sister to visit a college. It was nearby, just in Virginia, and we were gone half the day... But my phone died, and we were having fun. And when I got home, he was waiting for me, and he was angry. He'd called my parents and every friend I had. When everyone left, he methodically recounted all the ways he'd been worried about me. With his fists, with a belt, with whatever was around, honestly. I got nine stitches that night. All because my phone had died."

Alexi cursed and muttered under his breath even as he hung his head and shook it. "I'm so fucking sorry. I didn't even think about how you would react to my concern."

"And you shouldn't have to, because that is *my* thing. I reacted from the position of fear and defensiveness, I guess. I get now that you were concerned for my safety. Obviously, I understand that you're not going to hurt me. Because even though being with you feels like a free fall, I'm not scared of *you*. I'm scared of *how I feel* about you, and that's a completely different feeling than with Easton. I shouldn't have let it color how I interact with you."

"Let's face it, I went a little mental. I should have taken a step back and considered how you would feel. I just wanted you to be safe."

"Thank you. Because I now actually have someone who worries about me for the purposes of safety and well-being. If I didn't have all this baggage, I think it would probably have felt nice to be cared for."

"That's all I want. To care for you. And let's be honest. I'm in total freefall too. But I get that maybe I need to tone that down just a little. My life is complicated, and when I couldn't find you, I worried my life had encroached into yours."

I cocked my head. "What do you mean, complicated?"

His gaze searched mine. "We have a lot of time to talk about that. And I *do* want to talk about it. I think we should. But I don't want you to freak out. I know that you have reasons to worry, and I don't want to give you any more. I just want to be with you."

I shook my head. "And I want to be with you. More than I think I should."

He nodded slowly. "This happened really quickly, didn't it?"

"Yeah, you can say that again. I came to London to find myself and to escape. Next thing I know I'm pulled into your orbit and can't escape. And I'm pretty sure I don't want to."

He stepped toward me and took my hands. "I don't want you escaping either, but I get what you need to do. So maybe we pull back just a little. I can be patient."

I searched his gaze. "I want to do this, but maybe we *should* slow down just a little so I can get my bearings."

"I can do that. Maybe for now you just let me hold you, is that okay?"

I blinked back tears. "Yeah, that's very okay."

He tugged me forward and I met him halfway. "Now, that doesn't mean that I'm not going to still want to see you naked."

I laughed. "Ah, yeah. Do you want to go back for the towel? Because that was really working for me."

He chuckled softly. "I would very much like to entice you. But I think you're right. A slight pumping of the brakes is probably a good idea until both of us feel like were on a little more even footing."

I nodded. "I have a feeling I'm going to regret asking for that."

"So, I'll let you lead. As badly as I want to club you on the head, throw you over my shoulder and drag you into my bedroom, I am going to let you lead the way. You tell me what you're ready for."

I bit my bottom lip. "I want it all. I just... I think I have some work to do."

"Fair enough. But kissing is okay, right?"

"Hell, yes. Kissing, and touching. I just want to wrap my

mind around the pull we have. I'm not the only one who feels that, right?"

He shook his head. "No, I feel it too. And it is terrifying. But we're in it together. And I get it. You need time, and that's a really good idea. So, we can take our time."

"Excellent. In that case, maybe you can show me around? I've never been on a barge before."

"It will be my pleasure."

CHAPTER SIX

ALEXI

As it turned out, pumping the brakes didn't mean the urge to see each other diminished at all. If anything, it was worse. Last week, Abbie had come by the barge for a couple of hours, then I'd taken her home like a gentleman with minimal kissing, because Christ knew if I kissed her how I wanted, I'd be fucking her against the wall, and she needed time. And so did I to sort through the barrage of feelings.

I needed to figure out where I could find some patience because I was on edge.

When I arrived at her flat, she swung the door open with a grin. "Hi."

"Hello yourself."

My gaze swept over her. The red dress she wore was accented with African print on the edges. It hugged her waist, showing off her figure, with a peekaboo slit showing a hint of cleavage. She was going to kill me with that dress. "You look, sensational."

"You can pay me compliments anytime."

And then, I couldn't *not* be touching her. I wrapped my arms around her and picked her up off her feet, and she giggled. "Hello, beautiful."

"Hello, handsome. Are you ready for the surprise?"

I lifted a brow. "Now, when you said surprise, I have to tell you, I expected you to answer the door starkers."

She laughed. "You know, that's another kind of surprise, but I thought maybe you'd want to do a little something different."

"Well, I packed the necessities as you suggested." She had asked me to bring a suit. And a casual outfit. I dressed in a pair of Armani slacks and a light sweater. I knew the charcoal gray brought out the color in my eyes.

She gave me a brilliant smile. "You look very nice in casual."

"Wait until you see me in a suit." I nuzzled her neck, sliding my nose up the column of her throat and kissing just behind her ear. As the shiver ran through her body, I held on tighter. I tried to take a deep breath so I didn't rush her, but I was also aware my cock had zero chill and was nudging her belly.

"Mr. Chase, is that a giant penis in your pants, or are you just happy to see me?"

I pulled back and grinned. "Oh, it's a giant cock in my trousers."

Her gaze slid down and her eyes went wide. "Wow. Isn't he... enthusiastic?"

I groaned. "You can't look at him like that, love. Or then he really, *really* wants to come out and say hello. And that will pretty much shatter all our plans to take it slow."

She licked her lips, but then took a deliberate step back. "You're right."

She didn't stop looking at my dick though. "Woman, stop objectifying me for my large cock, and let's get somewhere public pronto."

She laughed. "Said no man ever. But we do have to get going. How do you walk around with that thing anyway?"

I blew out a breath and tried to think of Tottenham's football stats for the last year. That would surely depress me enough to deflate him. "That's just the normal state of affairs when I'm around you."

"How ever do you manage to walk around like a normal person?"

"It takes determination and mind over matter. Don't mind him. He'll be patient."

She studied me closely as she lifted her arms around my neck. "You're really okay with taking things slow?"

I nodded. "I am really okay about taking things as slowly as you want. Do I want you? Absolutely. Every second of the day. I think about you, and well, you can feel what happens. But I don't want you wary of me. I want you all in."

"How do you know 'all in' is what we should do?"

How in the world did I explain this feeling to her? "I just feel it. Don't worry. I'm patient." I kissed her nose. "Now where are we going?"

"The thing about Ghanaians is that we love celebrations. Weddings, funerals, outdoorings."

"What's an outdooring?"

"Oh, it's a way to introduce a child to the world and to give them their name."

"That sounds amazing."

"Yeah it's a big deal in Ghana. You invite people over. There's a big party. We're not going to an outdooring, but my cousin is getting married, and I have to go to her engagement party."

I nodded. "Well, I am dressed for the occasion, I assume?"

She nodded. "You look very nice."

She looked spectacular. Like one of the models Max worked with. "Why are you taller?"

She kicked out one of her feet to expose very high wedges.

I laughed. "Ah, that's why. It makes kissing you a little bit easier. But I like having you tucked in right here."

"Well, I liked how we fit too. But this is also nice. Our lips are closer together."

I nodded and then pulled her close to slide my lips over hers. "Yeah, I do like that."

"Good thing I didn't put my lipstick on yet. Otherwise, you'd be covered in red."

I lifted a brow. "Exactly where were you covering me with red?" I gave her a cheeky grin.

She laughed. "That is one distinct possibility. But we have to go."

"Okay, lead the way."

She grabbed her coat and her purse, and I let her lead me back down the stairs. "Mr. Chase, I can feel your eyes on my ass."

"What's a man to do? When the most beautiful woman in the world with the most incredible ass walks in front of him, he's going to look."

"Uh-huh. Maybe you can touch later."

When I reached the bottom of the stairs, I gave her a kiss on the nape of her neck. "Yes, but my girlfriend, she wanted to take it slow. So I'm trying to abide by her request."

She turned in my arms in the vestibule. "I said slowly. I didn't mean I wanted to fully halt this train."

I nodded. "Okay, in that case, why don't you define slow for me?"

"Well, let's see. I would very much like your lips on me."

I lowered my voice and pulled her even closer, my cock throbbing in my pants. "I like where this is going. Exactly where do you want my lips?"

"My neck. My lips."

I kissed her pulse, and I could feel it jump under my skin. "Is here good?"

Her moan was low. It sent a shiver of electricity through my body. "Is there anywhere else you'd like my lips?"

"Lower."

I nipped her gently with my teeth and pulled back. "I am shocked, Ms. Nartey. For you to suggest such a thing? I don't even know what to say."

She giggled. "You're teasing me."

I nodded. "Yes, I am. If you want my lips lower, you're going to have to tell me exactly where. We could play Marco Polo. Hot and cold. When I hit what you want, you just tell me in a nice low moan. How does that sound?"

"I like this version of going slow."

"How does this dress come off?"

"It's a very deadly zipper in the back."

I growled. "Go changed into a skirt. We can have fun at this engagement party."

"No, we have to go."

"How can you tease me and tell me I can still touch you and then not *let* me touch you?"

"It's called delayed gratification. Come on, let's go."

I groaned but followed behind her. "Woman, you're going to be the death of me."

"I'm sure you'll survive."

And maybe I would, but not without her taking a piece of my heart with her.

CHAPTER SEVEN

ABBIE

Relax. This isn't a test.

Who was I kidding? This was absolutely a test.

A test of how I could manage with Alexi in an environment where I'd only ever been with Easton. It was a test of how the two of us would interreact.

We'd been feeling each other out for the last week. And it was also a test for me. My immediate family wouldn't be there, but I wasn't a fool. Within five minutes of walking in with Alexi, there had been an auntie phone chain telling everyone who would listen that I'd walked into the engagement party with an oburoni, a white person.

But he'd been a trooper through the whole event.

Efua was one of twin cousins on my mother's side. We'd been close as kids, but I hadn't really seen her much in the last ten years or so. But thanks to that auntie phone tree, the expectation was that I would show up for the engagement party and wedding with gifts in tow.

It was hard to gauge Alexi's reaction. He'd seemed

surprised. I had told him it was an engagement party, and it was. But Efua's father was filthy rich. Gold and oil investments. So there were over a hundred and fifty people at the engagement party.

When we walked in, traditional dancers were performing, dressed in their Kente. Champagne rested in calabash basins all around the room on each of the tables. The bride-to-be and the groom were dancing.

Alexi's eyes went wide when the drummers came in. "Wow."

"Not what you expected?"

"I didn't know what to expect, but this is amazing."

"Yeah, isn't it? I'm sure her wedding will be another kind of spectacle too." He looked all around, taking it all in. "Do you have any African friends?"

He nodded. "My mate, Patrick. He's from Malawi. But he's never taken me to these kinds of parties before."

"I'm sure there will be some differences."

"This is amazing. Those dancers... Can you do that?"

I watched as the traditional dancers wound their hips in time to the drums. "Only a little. My mother stuck me in African dance classes when I was young. But really, all I wanted to dance to were pop songs. She was disappointed, of course. I really only started to get more into my culture as I went to Uni. I don't know why, but it became more important to me. For a while there, I only allowed people to call me Abena."

A waiter passed with glasses of champagne, and Alexi lifted two off the tray and handed me one. "Is that your preference?"

I shook my head. "I don't really have a preference. But through Uni, I don't know, I wanted to stamp more of my culture on my identity. I guess I was trying to differentiate myself from who other people *wanted* me to be."

He cocked his head. "Easton?"

I winced. "I don't really want to talk about my ex-boyfriend."

He shrugged. "You referencing him as being a twat doesn't bother me."

I laughed. "Okay. But still, he doesn't deserve my trips down memory lane."

"No, he doesn't."

When we sat down for food, Alexi stared at the menu cards. "Is it okay that I don't know what any of this is?"

"Yup. So, gari is this cassava derivative. It's a root vegetable. So it's ground, and normally, you add water or some kind of liquid to it, and then you eat it with stews and stuff like that. Gari foto is gari mixed with our tomato base stew."

"And what do they put in the stew?"

I shrugged. "I don't know. Basic stuff. Tomatoes, ginger, garlic, spices."

"Okay, in that case, I'm trying some of that."

"Well, you've had plantain before, right?"

He nodded. "Yeah, when I went to Puerto Rico for a while during a study-abroad program back when I was at Eaton."

"I think a lot of Puerto Ricans eat the unripe plantains, but these are the ripe ones fried in some oil."

We went along the options at the buffet table for food,

and he piled his plate high. I watched him carefully as he started sampling each bit. His eyes grew wide with each bite. "Oh my God, Abbie, this is amazing."

I grinned. "I know, right?"

"Can you make this stuff?"

"Yeah, most of it. I mean, some of the stews take longer. Like the okra stew. Ghanaian food is not made quickly."

"My God, a woman who can cook. And if you cook food like this, I should probably up my gym game so that I can eat it all."

"Oh, you think I'm going to make this for you?"

He nudged me gently. "I will do anything for more of this."

I laughed. "Well, luckily we're in London. I can find somebody to make most of this stuff."

"Fair enough. Why should my woman cook? You should rest on your laurels, and I can cater to you. Can you show me how to make this?"

My brows lifted. "You can cook?"

"Of course, I can cook. I have to eat. And I'm willing to learn."

"Why do I assume that you think I'm going to teach you to cook naked?"

He grinned. "I mean, a man can dream."

After we ate, I pulled him onto the dance floor. I knew from experience the man could move, so I didn't have to teach him how to find the beat. And he was completely game. He watched the people around us as we took hands and he matched my hip gyrations.

He was tall and lean, so he looked a little awkward doing

some of the moves, but he didn't seem to care. It was fun and easy, and God, I loved being with him. Everything about him made me smile and made me happy.

But still, my heart told me I needed to take it slow. Because what if one day this version of happy turned into something else?

He's not Easton.

I knew he wasn't Easton, but still, I couldn't help it. I couldn't help but worry about who he would become eventually. But I shoved those thoughts aside for another time.

Today, I could just enjoy being with him.

When the music changed from the more raucous hip-shaking music to something that was more high life and a bit of a slower tempo to allow the old folks to get on the dance floor, he still tucked me in his arms and held me tight as we danced.

"I have to say, I'm very impressed. You're one of the four white guys in the room, and none of this is making you uncomfortable at all?"

"Why should it? I'm getting a lesson on a part of you, why should I be uncomfortable?"

"NOT MANY PEOPLE could handle it, but you're taking it all in stride."

"I get to see a part of you. Of course, I'm taking in stride."

From behind me, a voice called out, "Abbie? Abena Nartey, is that you?"

I frowned and turned slowly in Alexi's arms. He still held on to me tightly and scowled. When I turned, I froze. "James."

"I thought that was you." Taking no notice of my partner, he wrapped his arms around me, despite my frozen stiffness. Then he backed off. "Jolly long time. Where's Easton? I thought he couldn't make it."

I swallowed hard. "Easton and I broke up, James."

James's face fell. "Oh, why? What did my cousin do?"

"It's not important. This is my—" Shit. I had no idea how to introduce Alexi.

But he stepped in easily. "Alexi Chase. I'm Abbie's date for the night."

James shook his hand but looked askance at him with a raised brow and a half-smile on his lips. "You brought this oburoni to a Ghanaian wedding?"

I lifted my chin. "He's my boyfriend."

Well, there it was.

James blinked. "He's your new boyfriend? And Easton has nothing to say about this?"

"Well, considering we broke up, no, not really. Now, if you'll excuse us." I didn't wait for a response. I just turned around, took Alexi's hand and marched him out into the hall. I just needed to get away. I needed air. I needed to breathe.

I knew I shouldn't have said boyfriend, but I wasn't going to let James insult him. Oburoni wasn't a bad term. All it meant was white person. But the inflection that James had added to it meant he didn't think Alexi belonged there. Didn't belong with me.

I had to get out of the crowd. I started walking and didn't stop until we neared the balcony. When we were finally out of the throng of people, I stopped and tried to catch my breath.

Alexi homed in on what was wrong right away. "Hey, I'm here. You can breathe. It's okay."

"I just need air. I just—"

He took my hand and tugged me out onto the balcony. "Hey, here we go. Nice and easy. Breathe. What's going on?"

I dragged in two deep breaths. "I didn't expect to see anyone who knew us both, you know? And that assumption that, of course, I would be with Easton just pissed me off, I guess. And I don't know... I just can't breathe."

He ran his hands up and down over my arms. "Easy does it. You want to tell me what oburoni means?"

"It just means white guy, or a white person."

"Well, I am white. Actually, I don't like white. I prefer melanin challenged."

And with that, I snorted a laugh. "How do you do that? Just dissipate whatever I'm feeling and make me feel better."

"I don't know. I know you. I care about you. I—" He stopped abruptly.

I watched him closely. He was going to say something else. "Yeah?"

He shook his head. "I care about you, so I'm in tune to what's going on with you. I also know how to make you laugh. That's going to happen a lot, Abbie. You're going to see people from your past at some point, and they're going to remind you that you're not with him anymore. Are you okay with that?"

"I don't know. It's the first time that's happened. I just feel scared. It's like the panic of just knowing that he might find out I was out with someone other than him and what it could mean."

"I get that. But you don't have to be afraid. I'm here. And even if I wasn't, you're strong. I'm quite certain you don't even need me."

I shook my head. "I do."

He shook his head to argue with me. "No. I like to think that you *want* me here. But you don't *need* me. You are stronger than you even know. That scared girl who Easton tormented? She's gone. He can't hurt you anymore. And that's *your* doing, not mine. I just happen to be able to reap the benefits of you learning the power of your own strength. I'm pretty sure I would have liked you either way, but I particularly like this version of you. You were brave enough to get out. Brave enough to move halfway across the world, brave enough to tell him to go fuck off. You're strong. I watched you stand up to the worst kind of bully in defense of someone else. You're stronger than you knew you were."

"What did I ever do to deserve you?"

He brushed a thumb over my cheek. "You are just being beautiful and fantastic. I'm the lucky one. I stumbled on to you and I'm just trying to keep up and be the best version of me so you don't realize that I'm the lucky one and ditch me."

"Something tells me I won't be ditching you for a very, very long time, Mr. Chase."

"Oh, I'm depending on that."

CHAPTER EIGHT

ALEXI

W ine, check. Pasta, check. I had everything I needed. I was going to make her dinner tonight.

And you're totally smitten.

She was right. Things had moved quickly, and she needed time. So I was determined to give her as much time as possible. Time to be exactly what she needed me to be. I could see how I'd freaked her out. I could do this though.

I gathered the makings for dinner outside of my car and then juggled the bags as I headed toward the barge. I stepped up to find my neighbor, Killian, waving at me. "All right, mate?"

I smiled up at him. "When did you get back?"

"Just this morning. I thought I saw your lights on, so I popped by to say hello, but you weren't there."

Killian and I had been neighbors for a couple of years now. Every now and again, he'd leave out for parts unknown before eventually coming back. He was a good bloke. And we'd had more than a glass of wine to celebrate our adventures before.

"Nope, I haven't been home. I'm making dinner for someone special tonight."

"Oh, you pretty boys."

I laughed. Killian was around thirty-five, maybe a little older. Wiser. He'd been in love once, but apparently that hadn't gone well, so he'd retreated to his barge. And every time I saw him, I'd come by and visit. Sometimes I figured he might be lonely, but then he'd be off once again to parts unknown, traveling. God, I hoped that wasn't me one day. I hoped to have some people in my life who forced themselves and their company on me at some point.

"Oh, to be young and in love. Maybe one of these days you'll bring your lady on by to meet me."

"Sure, we could have dinner. Wine. We can work it out before the weather gets too bad."

"Got to love all of this sunshine. I feel like we're dooming ourselves for the winter."

"All right, mate. Well, let me get inside. I need to cook."

He nodded. "Go on then."

I fumbled my keys into the lock only to find that the door was slightly ajar. I frowned.

What the hell?

I kicked open the door. Was it possible I hadn't shut it firmly behind me? Anything was possible. I put the bags down and hung up my coat and then pushed the door into the main space. It was the only way to keep the heat trapped in. When I shoved open the secondary door, I frowned. *Son of a bitch.* Killian had seen the light on, all right. Because someone had fucking ransacked the place. It was a complete mess. My couch had been slashed. Family photos yanked off the wall. Glass shattered on the ground.

I knew the smart thing was to back up, get back to the car, and call the police. But I couldn't help myself. I started a slow perusal. Someone had been there. What were they looking for? Step by step, I cautiously looked around the living room and dining area.

When I first bought the barge, I'd expanded the kitchen. I turned the entire bottom floor into an open concept. Had the whole barge refitted. Now, there were slash marks on my cabinets.

Son of a bitch.

I didn't know if anything was gone. I'd had my laptop in the car with me, as I'd come straight from work. I eased toward the bedroom, listening, but there was nothing. No sound. No indication of an intruder.

There was a backdoor to the barge. Really, it led from the bedrooms on to what I call sort of a patio, my little garden area. Someone could have easily escaped out the back without Killian ever seeing them.

The beds were tossed, pillows slashed, and there were feathers everywhere. Fuck.

The first thing I did was call Abbie. I didn't need her seeing this. When she answered on the first ring, she had a smile in her voice. "Hey, I was just going to head out in a little bit. I was going to shower first. What do you want me to bring?"

My stomach coiled and knotted when she spoke. "Yeah,

actually, there's been a change of plans. I'm going to take you out to dinner instead."

She paused. "Everything okay?"

"Yeah, I thought maybe we'd go out and then head to Max's place. It is technically movie night."

"Uh, I thought we'd be having a date night."

Fuck. She wanted alone time, which I very much did, too. But I couldn't have her here now. "Let's meet there, and we can decide on the plan."

"Sure. Yeah, let me just, uh, quickly shower and throw on some jeans and stuff."

I swallowed hard. "Okay, I'll meet you at Max's."

"Yeah. Are you okay? You sound weird."

"Yeah, I'm fine. Just, you know, a lot on my mind. I'll see you soon."

"Okay."

The police were my next call. I wouldn't be sticking around to deal with them, though. I had security for that, and they were who I called next. They'd come down and run through this situation with the police. I didn't have time for that. I needed to see Abbie. I knew it was ridiculous, but I wanted to make sure she was okay.

Ease up. You're going to smother her to death.

I knew I was overdoing it. She'd as much as said so the other night. I just couldn't help it. But what if I'd brought her home and someone had stepped out in there?

Fuck.

After the call to security, I immediately made calls to Jean Claude and Xander too. I told my brother to watch his back and checked in with Jean Claude to make sure he didn't know anything about this. He denied it, of course, but it was worth a shot.

Even as I left my barge, a prickle of unease tripped over my skin. I glanced around but saw nothing untoward. Killian was still on his deck. "All right, mate?"

I nodded. "Yeah. Actually, since you're here, I have security coming down. They're going to meet the police."

Killian frowned. "Why?"

"Well, it seems someone broke in. That must have been the light you saw."

He groaned. "Oh, mate, sorry. I didn't know. I only pulled in about an hour ago."

"No big deal. It's just things, right?"

"Well, thank God you weren't home or didn't have your lady-friend over."

"Yeah. Thank God. Um, so that's what's up if anyone asks questions."

'Right. I got you. Did they take anything?"

"I didn't even check. Nothing important."

"Right. As long as you have your life. That's all that matters."

Yeah, the problem was that I couldn't be sure if someone was trying to fuck with it or take it.

ABBIE...

I quickly tied my braids up. I was a little disappointed we weren't going to be at Alexi's. It was unusual for him to change plans on me. He'd sounded off. Which only made me worry that something was wrong and he didn't want me to know.

Stop being paranoid.

What would Dr. Kaufman say? I had to keep reminding myself that he wasn't Easton. And while he was all the things I'd been pretty sure I didn't want, he was also kind and sweet and generous.

It was fine. We'd go eat, and then we'd hang out with Sophie and everyone. I didn't want to be one of those girls who had a new boyfriend and then vanished on her friends. So, I could do this. Hang with the crew, even though I was desperate to spend some time with him. I knew I'd been the one to say that I wanted to take things slow, but we hadn't made love since the night after the garden party. We'd kissed, but not much else. And he was respecting my wishes, I knew, but damn, I liked him touching me.

What terrified me was how easy it was to get drawn into his orbit. His charisma, his charm, that gravitational pull, the feeling that he was who I belonged with, that was the scary part. Because it would be easy to lose myself again. Easy for him to hurt me.

He's not Easton.

With a deep breath and a shake of my head, I grabbed my overnight bag, just in case, and headed down the stairs of the flat. When I pushed open the door, a bite of wind slid into my scarf, chilling me to the bone.

Dammit. I supposed the bout of good weather we'd been enjoying was about to be over.

I pulled out my phone to see the best route. I could just take the bus. Or I could call for a car to take me door to door.

Or I could take the tube, which would be saving money. Because I still didn't have a damn job.

Or I could just take ease and comfort.

No, I would take the tube. The tube station was just a little over a quarter of a mile away. It was fine.

Mrs. Combs, our next-door neighbor to the right, smiled and waved at me. "Good evening, love."

"Hello, Mrs. Combs. How are you?"

"Oh, you know, just a little pain in my back. It's best if I get some exercise."

She walked around her small garden, picking her vegetables. I'd never even pictured myself having a neighbor like her. One I could chat to, who would have invited me in for tea. But here I was with a lovely elderly neighbor whose name I knew and who knew mine but instead preferred to call me love. I was becoming a proper Brit.

It had drizzled earlier, but the rain had stopped. But as the cars whizzed by on Grove Park Gardens, the tires all made splashing sounds as they drove through puddles.

As per usual, I put in one of my earbuds, leaving the other open so I could hear my surroundings. No point in being stupid just because I wanted to listen to some good music.

As I walked, a tingle ran up my spine and I looked around. It was that same feeling I'd had in Notting Hill the day I ran into Xander. What was wrong with me?

Besides an abusive ex, nothing. Yeah, but he was in my rear view. And in this new life, I didn't have to be afraid of everything.

Something told me I'd be telling myself that for a long time to come.

The further I walked, the worse the feeling got. It raised the hair on my arms. I could feel the impending panic attack. My heart rate increased. My breathing was shallower with every step, as if my body was trying to force me to stop, turn back around, and run inside.

The tube wasn't that far away. I could do this. Or maybe I should just give up and call a car.

No, you're not going to call a car. You don't have the money.

And I was being silly. One lap around the track. That's as far as I had to go.

Plus, I didn't want to have to explain to Mrs. Combs why I was running back to my flat and locking the door behind me.

Suck it up, let's go.

I forced my feet to march.

Up ahead, a car idled. I was trying to figure out if I recognized it or not, but there were so many houses on the road, some mansions, some cottages that had been split into flats like the one Faith and I lived in. There was no way of telling what was familiar and what wasn't.

But still, as I approached the car, my heart squeezed. My gut knotted. Whatever lizard part of my brain still existed, screamed, *Run. Go back. Go back now.*

But I couldn't run. My feet were rooted to the ground. I was stuck. Frozen. The driver's side door opened, and I stopped breathing. Long legs. Strong pair of arms. Trim body.

Tall. Smooth, dark brown skin. Perfectly trimmed beard. My breathing came in shallow puffs. "Easton?"

To my own ears, my voice sounded wary and tremulous, like I could cry at any moment. When I blinked rapidly, the moisture told me tears were already on the verge of spilling over.

His face was impassive. "Do you know how hard I had to look for you?"

Run. Move. Scream. Anything. Just do anything.

But I couldn't do any of those things. I was stuck. Stuck in my life. Stuck on the street. I couldn't move forward, but I refused to move backward.

I had no weapons, nothing but my body, toiletries for the night and my phone. I forced myself to speak. "What are you doing here?"

"I'm here to take you home. This little adventure... It's over."

I shook my head. "No, I'm not going with you."

His brow furrowed. "Listen. I'm done fighting with you. I've given you your space. You don't like it that I took your passport? Fine. You'll get over it. But you're coming home. I've had enough."

"I'm not going anywhere with you."

His lips set into a firm line as he glanced around. "Abena, don't make a scene. Get in the fucking car."

I shook my head. "No." And then came a surge of strength. My phone buzzed in my hand, and I glanced down. There was a text from Alexi. *Are you sure you want to take the tube? I can just come pick you up.*

At that moment, I understood what Dr. Kaufman had been trying to tell me. While Alexi might be possessive, and while he might overreact and call the police when I didn't turn up, he wasn't this man in front of me. This man wanted to smother me. This man wanted to hurt me. This man wanted to own me, and while Alexi wanted to possess me, there was a part of him that admired me for demanding what I needed from him, a part of him that wanted me to be free. They were different. I'd been hiding from them both, but they were different. I had wasted time being afraid of my feelings for Alexi. I tilted my chin up and glared at Easton. "If you want me in that car, you're going to have to put me in it. Because as sure as hell, I'm *not* getting in voluntarily." And then his cool and calm facade was gone. It slipped as if a mask had been lifted. The snare was quick, as were his movements. Three steps to me and he was grabbing my shoulders. "You think I can't control you? Get in the fucking car."

"No. I feel like we've already been through this once. You can physically force me in the car. You can take me if you want, but I will always fight you. I will never come willingly. And one day, you will have to rest, and I will kill you in your sleep. So Let. Me. Go."

His brows lifted, and he blinked rapidly. I'd never fought back before. Sure, I'd cowered, and begged, and ran away, but I'd never fought, except for that last night in the flat. And that last night in the flat had taught me so much. That I could and was capable of fighting back.

"Shut up." He squeezed my shoulders hard and tried to pull me to the car, but I fought.

"Help!"

I fought his hold, and he started to drag me. I screamed. "Mrs. Combs. Mrs. Combs!"

I fought and whacked him with my bag and kicked. A smack on my cheek with the back of his hand stung and startled, but it didn't stop me.

I screamed louder.

Finally, the man two doors down from Mrs. Combs came stomping out of his house. I didn't know his name, but he said good morning to me whenever I headed out for early morning photo shoots. He was some kind of construction worker. He had tools on his truck and always had a tool belt and a fluorescent vest he wore. "Oi. What's happening?"

Easton scowled in his direction. "Mind your own business."

The man crossed his arms and glared at Easton. But then he shifted his gaze to me. "Are you all right, love?"

I shook my head. "No. Not all right."

He pulled out his phone and dialed the police. "Mate, you're going to let her go."

Easton started shoving me faster and turned to pull the backseat door open.

I kicked him in the shins and ran for my savior, standing behind him. Easton tried to grasp me, and grabbed my bag, but I happily let it go.

"Abena, get back here."

"You're going to have to go through him if you want me."

For a moment I thought Easton was going to, and then poor, sweet Mrs. Combs ventured out onto the sidewalk. "Dear? Are you all right?"

"No, I'm not all right. This guy tried to shove me in his car."

Easton could see the lay of the land now. He tried to jump in the driver's seat, but the hulking man in front of me ran and stopped him. "Nah, mate. The police are already on their way."

In the distance, I could hear the sirens.

Easton was furious. His anger mask slid on. The one where his face didn't move, but the tick of his jaw was unmistakable. He wanted to hurt me. But he wasn't going to get the chance. I had neighbors and people who cared about me. I didn't have to go with him. I didn't have to be that girl anymore.

The police were quick to arrive, and my savior basically stood in front of Easton's car door and wouldn't move. Once the police were there, I could feel the tightness unfurling in my chest. I was safe. I didn't have to be that scared girl anymore. He couldn't hurt me ever again.

CHAPTER NINE

ABBIE

I was late. *An hour and a half late.* And since I'd been talking to the police, I hadn't been able to text or call.

Knowing Alexi, he was probably ready to call the police again himself.

I shivered thinking about how I'd spent the last hour and a half. Recounting all the ways Easton had hurt me.

When I rang the doorbell, I had to wait a moment before the door finally opened. Jasper met me with a wide grin. "My day just started looking up. Hello, beautiful." He enveloped me in a hug.

I couldn't even return it. I just stood stiffly at the doorway, too shell-shocked for anything else. He didn't even notice that it was the police that dropped me off.

When he backed off, he frowned. "You okay?"

I nodded slowly. "Is Alexi here?" My voice was soft and slightly hoarse. I didn't even know how I hadn't been crying as I was speaking with the police. I just couldn't muster the energy.

Alexi practically growled from somewhere behind Jasper. "Jasper, let her go."

Jasper rolled his eyes. "Possessive, that one." He backed up and stepped aside for me to come in. Alexi came into view, and I could feel my chest start to loosen and relax. He frowned when he noticed the police lights outside.

"Did something happen to one of the neighbors?"

I shook my head. "They're for me."

He scowled "What's happened?"

My gaze flickered to Jasper, who was studying us. "Um, it's fine. Can we just... can everyone just watch the movie?"

Jasper didn't look like he wanted to leave, but Alexi turned to him and lifted a brow. Jasper rolled his eyes. "Fine. I'm gone."

When he retreated, I turned back and waved at the officers who'd dropped me off. Lex didn't immediately wrap me in his hold, but he took my hand. "Why don't you tell me what happened?"

"I—"

He closed the door behind me first, then shook his head. "Okay, sorry. Let's do this right. Come here into the kitchen." He took my bag from me, settled it on one of the chairs, and then reached into my jacket to my shoulders and slid the coat off of me.

He placed it on the back of a chair and then turned on the kettle. He took my hand and led me to a chair. My knees were so tired and weak that I couldn't do anything but sit. He pulled out another chair and seated himself across from me and took my hands. "Okay, what's wrong?"

What was I going to say? I'm a complete fucking mess?

That was the truth. I *was* a mess. With a psycho ex-boyfriend to boot. But I didn't want Easton to own my story. I didn't want him to take any part of my life in London. In the end, I had no choice but to just say the truth. "I was leaving the flat, and then Easton showed up." I couldn't even look at Alexi. Seeing the anger on his face would only terrify me, so I just hurried on. "He tried to pull me into his car. The neighbors helped me. The police came. He's been arrested."

When I glanced up, there was no anger on Alexi's face. His voice was soft. "Did he hurt you?"

"I— No, I'm not hurt. I'm just scared."

He pulled me close. "I'm so sorry I wasn't there for you."

"It's not your fault. I've just been going about my business for weeks, feeling like someone's following me. And I just— I should have paid attention. I was so stupid. I *did* this. God, I'm such a mess."

"You're not a mess. This has nothing to do with you. I think it all makes sense why we're here now."

I frowned up at him. "I don't understand."

"Sweetheart, I'm so sorry. I should have come to get you. Our date was ruined tonight because someone broke into the barge."

I blinked up at him. "What?"

He nodded slowly. "Seeing as Easton tried to grab you off the street, I have the distinct impression it might have been him."

I tried to pull out of his arms, but he didn't let me.

"Alexi, let me go. This is my fault. I'm ruining your life."

"Are you kidding me? You're the best thing that has happened in my life."

"My ex-boyfriend legitimately broke into your place."

"*If* he did, I'll have him on the security camera. The police have already been called, and my security people are taking care of it. It's okay. He'll get charges filed against him. And then he'll get deported, and you'll be safe."

"Don't you get it, I'm not safe anywhere. I go to a wedding, and there's his family. And what happens someday when I need to go home and see *my* family? He's the son of a diplomat. An arrest won't mean much. He'll be summoned home because of the embarrassment. But he'll eventually be able to come back."

"We'll see about that when the time comes. But for right now, you are in my arms and you are safe. Nothing is going to hurt you."

I wanted to believe him. I *wanted* to burrow into the warmth of his embrace and stay there. Let him keep me safe. I wanted to believe everything that he said. But, how could I? I wasn't safe. Easton wasn't just letting me go. And he certainly wasn't going to let me get away with having a new boyfriend and having a new life. "Will the police let him go?"

Alexi smoothed his hand over my hair. "Hey, I know what you're thinking. I'm going to make a couple of calls, okay? I promise you. If there was ever a time to throw my family's weight around, this is the moment."

"I don't want you to do that for me. Because of me, your life is tossed upside down."

"No, because of you, I've been able to feel something for the first time in a long time. That's worth the inconvenience of having to hire cleaners and get a new couch."

I frowned. "Why do you have to get a new couch?"

"Uh, let's just say my other one is damaged."

"Do I even want to know?"

He shook his head. "Nope. It's not important. I'm going to have you stay at the barge. The cleaners will take a couple of days, tops. And then you'll come stay with me for a night or two. I'm going to have new locks installed, a new security system, the whole thing. It will be really safe, I swear."

"I'm not worried about the safety of your barge. I'm worried that someone broke in because of me."

He shook his head. "No. Let's put the blame where it belongs."

I sighed and nodded.

"So, he could have just as easily decided that you were dating Xander. He could have easily ransacked *your* flat, right?"

"Yeah, but that doesn't—"

"The point is the blame lies with *him,* not you. You've moved on. You left him. And I'm so proud of you. This is on him. Put the blame on his shoulders."

The kettle started to whistle, and he set me back on my seat and turned around to grab mugs off the hooks that were hanging low over the stove. "Now, I'm going to make you the kind of tea that you like. You know, a splash of tea with your sugar."

I coughed a laugh. "Why are you being so nice to me?"

"Well, because someone needs to show you what it's like when someone actually cares about you. So, right now, I'm going to make my girlfriend some tea. And then I'm going to hold her if she'll let me. And maybe when she's ready, we'll go downstairs and finish watching the movie. It's going to be simple. And that way, you don't have to talk to anyone or explain anything, right?"

I searched his gaze. He understood. I didn't want to have to explain anything. I didn't want to have to talk. I needed time to process, and I just wanted to be held in his arms.

I nodded. "I don't know what I did to deserve you."

"I promise you, I'm the one who got the better end of this deal."

CHAPTER TEN

LEX

Dance music thrummed through my ears as I surveyed the crowd at Lace Nightclub. Judging by the waitresses' outfits, leather and chains and not much else were an integral part of the uniform. So was lace, like the name suggested.

Leaning into Gemma and Nick, I shouted, "One of you want to remind me what I'm doing here again? Gemma this was hardly what I meant when I said I wanted to talk to you."

Nick rolled his eyes. "Don't be arsy that I crashed your party. Gem said you were meeting for a drink, so I invited myself along. Just like Uni."

It was just like Uni. Nick usually tagging along. "Maybe I wanted something quiet."

He raised a brow at me as if calling me out on my hypocrisy. He knew something was up with Abbie. We hadn't been fooling anyone with the 'Hey I'm worried about her because she's late to teach me photography,' thing. And he'd known for a bit something was very off with Gemma. He just was mate enough not to press.

He knew I'd talk when I wanted to. "Man, you can't be a recluse all your life. You have to go out. Or has something been keeping you busy? Besides, we have reason to celebrate. Or haven't you heard? We're rich."

I shook my head. "We were rich before. Just now, it's with our own money. And you know there is work that comes with that right?" And lots of it. Between the sale of our company and the additional boost from my trust fund, I would be richer than my father.

"Richer. Whatever. Still a reason to celebrate."

"I'll celebrate when I find a new CEO. Until then, I prefer to keep a low profile."

"Whatever, mate. You can sit here with your girl and mope all you want. I'm going to go and find someone nice and dangerous and see if I can coax her into spanking me."

I assessed the raven-haired beauty clad in head-to-toe black leather that Nick stared at. "Something tells me it won't take much to convince her."

Nick grinned as he followed the wannabe dominatrix, and I could only laugh. "Remind me again why I'm friends with him?" I asked Gemma.

"Because, despite his many failings, he's a good friend. And he worries about you. About us. He never asks too many questions, but he knows." She took a sip of her drink. "So, what's the big emergency? I've been busy this week. But the real question is what in the world have you been up to? I haven't seen *you* in weeks. I'm starting to worry you're depressed or something. You can't just hide away from the world."

I hadn't exactly been hiding away. I'd just been spending every spare minute I could with Abbie, playing undercover couple. So far, no one had taken any notice of us. Riding public transport with her and doing normal people things like schlepping groceries, and hanging out in the public gardens, and seeing museums were a great way to go unnoticed. I'd never given it much thought before, but there was a way to avoid the limelight, and that was to not court it. Whether I liked it or not, club hopping with my friends made me an easy target. So far, we'd been lucky. But things could spiral out of control easily.

I'd been out with Abbie on her shooting expeditions, and so far, not one person had recognized me. Even the gossip-hungry teenagers we'd encountered once at the Basingstoke Mall, where she'd wanted to hit up a boutique to get Faith a present for her upcoming birthday, hadn't seemed to recognize me. And it wasn't like my disguise had been that good.

It made me wonder if the company I kept was the main reason for all the fanfare over the last several years. After all, we'd usually turn up, the whole crew. Max and the lads. Chock full of actors and models and my brother, and well, yes. We were a magnet. But individually we weren't that interesting.

"I'm not depressed, Gem. I've just been busy."

She studied me closely, her pale blue eyes assessing me. "Okay, what gives? There's something different about you. You're relaxed. For as long as I've known you, there's always been this edginess to you. It's still there, but you're not as hard, I guess. Does that even make sense?"

"I feel good. Listen, things have been changing for me. And—"

"Oh my God. Are you actually getting shagged regularly? Even Jacinda has been noticing that I've been distracted, worrying about you."

"I don't think regularly is the word I'd used, but I met someone and—"

She smacked my arm. "I'm so happy for you."

A warm flush swept through me. She was one of my best mates, so of course she'd be happy. "Thanks, but that means that we need to rethink everything. I want to make a go of it with this girl. Our thing is so messy. But I don't want to hang you out to dry. I just need to start living. For real."

Her pale blue gaze searched mine. "All good things must come to an end, right? Jacinda will be happy."

"What exactly is going on there, anyway?" Things seemed solid with Gemma and Jacinda. I didn't want to keep hiding things from Abbie. She'd practically bared her soul to me, and I was still keeping secrets. The need to come clean made me twitchy. But I wanted to take care of my friend before I spilled all her secrets too.

Gemma shrugged, and her brightness suddenly turned somber. "Not sure. She's fully out of the closet. Her parents, her friends, her colleagues. I'm so fully in the closet that I've got a Blahnik shoved up my ass. It's taking a toll, and I'm not sure how long I can keep it casual." She smoothed a hand over her hair. "How serious are you two?"

The question had my gut twisting. "It's complicated, Gem. But I want it. I think maybe it's time to call this thing."

She practically gulped the rest of her drink. "She makes you happy, so I'm happy for you, but it's already complicated, and it pays to be careful. I need to deal with my parents and stuff. Find another situation before we go public. I'll need somewhere to hide so Dad doesn't shove young solicitors and bankers at me."

I knew what Gemma was trying to tell me. "Or you could just tell him the truth and not hide."

She shook her head. "You know what he's like. My life will literally be over."

I scrubbed a hand down my face. "You are still always welcome at my place. That doesn't change. I have a spare bedroom. You will never be out on the street."

"And how well do you think that's going to go over with your girlfriend?"

"She'll understand. Once we explain—"

She shook her head. "No. No one knows. I need to keep it that way. Just give me a little more time. That's all I'm asking. And I'm asking you not to tell your girl. You trust her, but it's my life so I don't want her to know."

"I get it, Gem. But I hate lying. And you and I have been living half-lives. Don't you want a full life, Gem?"

"It's different for you." Tucking her hair behind her ear, she asked. "Give me two more weeks, then we can do a break-up statement or something."

I lifted a brow. "A statement?"

"Yeah. To get ahead of the PR."

I sighed not wanting to push too much. "Fine. But we

need to do it. I don't want to wait anymore. I've told enough lies as it is."

She blinked rapidly, holding back what looked like impending tears. I'd hold her, but I knew she didn't want that. She'd take it as pity.

"I'm okay, Lex. I was going to have to become a big girl sooner or later."

"I know. I just didn't want to abandon you."

"You're not. I promise. I've stopped us both from living long enough."

I didn't want to agree with her, no matter how true it was. Our arrangement had been convenient once. But it was stale and serving neither of us well anymore.

I scanned the crowd. Apparently, kink didn't scare off the young, elite, and rich. The usual crowd I'd see at China White were all here trying too hard not to look desperately bored. Through the crowd, I spotted a flashbulb go off, and I stiffened.

Calm down, mate. Of course, the club had hired photographers for the event. But I eyed the shutterbug again. Slight build. Dirty blond hair gelled up into spikes. I could have sworn I'd seen him before. The hairs on the back of my neck stood at attention, but I couldn't place the guy. I needed to calm down. The hiring staff would only hire reputable photographers. They knew that we required the utmost privacy, and they wouldn't hire anyone who had ever worked with the tabloids. But still, I couldn't shake the feeling I'd seen the guy before. Maybe he was one of Xander's students?

"Speaking of complications..." I muttered. I couldn't have missed Abbie's entrance with her friends if I'd been trying.

Sophie squealed when she spotted me, and immediately a flock of women swarmed the models. One of the guys put his arm around Abbie, and I had the irrational urge to plant my fist in his face.

She'd texted earlier to say she was going out, but I had no idea she'd end up here.

As always, she looked stunning. She'd worn her braids piled on top of her head in some kind of bun, with long dangling earrings showing off her slender neck.

Gemma glanced toward the entrance. "Given the electric sparks between you two across a room, I see why the urgency."

"Leave it, Gem."

"Just saying. Give me a couple of weeks before you two get cited for public eye shagging." She gathered up her purse. "I think I'll go see what Nick's up to."

I didn't even see which way she went because my attention was so focused on Abbie. And as if she felt my eyes on her, she immediately looked up.

When our gazes locked, need chased the elation through my veins. I'd only seen her yesterday, but any time I spent away from her felt like eons. But it wasn't like I could really complain. She'd had work to do for my brother. I tried not to think about what Xander had said about her. It didn't matter what Xander thought. I couldn't stop seeing her.

She climbed the stairs, her soft skirt swishing against her legs as she did. When she reached the landing, she fixed me with a smile. "Fancy meeting you here." She looked around surreptitiously. "In a sex club."

"Oh, is it a sex club? I hadn't noticed." I grinned. "Nick's idea."

"Ahh, he didn't really strike me as the whips-and-chains kind of guy." She shrugged.

For several moments, we stood facing each other, neither moving, forcing anyone who wanted access to the stairs to go around us. Finally, I angled my body a little closer to her and said, "It's one of his dad's clubs. Do you want to go somewhere a little more private... to talk?"

Her eyes flashed. "Yeah." She cleared her throat. "Talking seems like a really good idea, actually."

I took her hand and led her through the throngs of the VIP section, past the dominatrix with her victim for the night, and past the sex viewing rooms. She held on tight to me as we passed by them.

"Are they having..."

"Yeah." As much as I wanted to be with her, I hated having her here in the midst of all the kink that was going on. "Maybe we should leave the club?"

"I—No. It's okay. We came as a group for Jasper's gig tonight. Apparently, there's some big promoter here. Jasper's hoping to get some representation tonight. We're sort of supporting him. Everyone would notice if I left."

"Right." *Jasper*. Jasper might be my friend, but jealousy ate at me. I wanted her there to support me. Of course, I'd have to tell her something real about myself first. I found the private rooms, then after looking around to make sure no one paid us any attention, I dragged her inside. Dim red light illuminated the comfortable-looking couch and bed. Her eyes widened as she glanced around. "This is... cozy."

I kissed her softly, and for a moment, all the tension ebbed out of my body. "I just wanted to be alone with you for two minutes before things get crazy out there and we don't have a minute to talk all night."

"No. It's fine." She placed a hand on my chest, and my heart hammered. "I'd rather get a minute with you, even if it's in a sex room. I wanted to talk to you about something."

We'd spent a lot of time together over the last week, but we hadn't been *alone*. Always out in public. Even the photo lab had been occupied when I'd gone to help her. The one night we'd made a date for her to go to my place, she'd had to do some schoolwork for Xander and rescheduled. The prick of guilt stung as I thought of how badly her last critique had gone.

"Okay, talk." I kissed the crook of her neck and inhaled. Her perfume, mixed with her unique scent, drove me a little crazy and made my head swim.

"Alexi, I can't—" She moaned when I licked her. "I can't think when you're doing that."

"Okay, sorry." I drew back. "Sometimes I forget to slow down."

She blinked up at me and inhaled deeply. "Sometimes I don't want you to."

I stilled. *What?* "I don't understand."

"Have you noticed that even after we said we'd ease up on intensity we've been spending every minute we can together?"

Something ominous and slimy squirmed in my gut. "I thought that was a good thing."

"It is. Maybe we don't need to take it quite so slow anymore."

Relief washed over me like a wave. As did panic. I was totally fucked. I was completely in love with her. And there were things she still didn't know about me.

"You're okay with this?"

She nodded. "I want you." She shook her head. "I get it now. This feeling is unlike anything I've ever felt before."

I pulled her in and kissed her because I couldn't bear not to. My tongue slid over hers in the familiar pattern, and my blood thickened. She responded by winding her hands into my hair and tugging me close. I'd been half hard from the moment she walked into the club, but now my erection throbbed insistently behind the fly of my jeans.

As my hands slipped under her shimmery top to feel the satin-smooth skin beneath, Abbie moaned into my mouth. My thumbs traced each rib, and she melted against me. Her breath caught when her belly came into contact with the thick length of me.

Fuck. My body kept screaming, *there is a bed right here,* and she clearly wanted me. But we didn't have time for this. Our friends would miss us.

Very deliberately, I placed my hands on her hips. I held her tight for several seconds, wanting to drag her closer and grind my dick into her to show her how much I wanted her. To hint that I knew just what that bed was for and had an idea where all the sex toys might be. Instead, I set her a foot away from me and my stiff erection.

We both dragged in gulps of air. Her eyes were cloudy and hooded as she blinked up at me. "Wh-why'd you stop?"

I tried desperately to clear my brain of lust and think clearly. "What?"

"Don't stop." She took a step toward me.

I stepped back. If I touched her again, I might not be able to stop myself. "Abbie, we're not doing this here. As much as I want to be with you, I really don't want a rushed quickie in a sex room."

She nodded slowly and inched forward. "So, you still want me?"

I dragged my hands through my hair. "Jesus. I'm trying desperately to be the good guy. I'm trying very hard to not drag you into that bed and peel off your top to see if you're wearing a bra over those pretty tits of yours. How can you ask if I still want you? I've been dreaming about you every night. You're all I've been able to think about the last couple of weeks."

She reached for me, unbuttoning my top button, then the next, and all the way down until my shirt hung open. When her fingertips brushed my skin, I squeezed my eyes shut, trying to manage the deluge of need. She was touching me like she needed me, like she would die if she didn't have me. So what was my problem?

"Fuck it," I muttered as I dragged her to me again, melding my lips with hers. I pushed my tongue inside her sweet warmth, desperate to taste her. Needing to know how much she wanted me.

She responded by sucking on my tongue, sliding hers, so wet and so hot, against mine that my knees wobbled. When she pressed her body flush against mine, I couldn't think.

I lifted her so she straddled my hips, and I braced her

against the wall. I was desperate to bury myself inside her, but I wasn't going anywhere near that bed. She held onto my shoulders and locked her legs behind my back. Devouring her mouth, I slid my hands back up her torso until my thumbs skimmed across bare breast.

I dragged my mouth from hers. "Fuck, Abbie, I was kidding about the no-bra thing."

Her answering smile was feminine and powerful. "You like the look?"

"God, yes." I hated the idea of any of the blokes she came with getting a peek down her blouse, but it was so sexy. I palmed both of her breasts, and she tossed her head back, baring her neck. Leaning over, I nipped then licked at a sensitive spot on the column of her throat before sucking on it gently, marking her as mine.

My thumbs and forefingers pinched her nipples, and she moaned my name while rocking her hips against me. "Lex, please..."

"I know what you need." I placed open-mouth kisses along her throat until I reached her lips again. I removed one hand from her breast and massaged the back of her neck as I kissed her.

I let her legs fall back to the floor and wedged a knee between her thighs. She moaned at the contact. I knew by now how close she was. Her little mewling sounds were a dead giveaway. "That's it, Abbie. Help me make you feel good. Show me how you like it. Ride me. Move how you want." I pinched her nipple again, and she screamed.

I lifted the soft material of her blouse, exposing her blackberry-tipped nipples. Unable to help myself, I lowered my head to one of the darkened buds. Right before wrapping my lips over the puckered tip, I whispered, "You are so beautiful."

The moment I licked her, she trembled then came apart in wild convulsions. I didn't let up, sucking her nipple, drowning in her need. She rode my leg, and her thigh brushed my groin on every movement of her hips. Each movement was pure torture, and I was certain I'd never sleep tonight.

"Oh, God, Alexi." Another orgasm rolled through her, and I watched in wonder. When she came, she was the picture of pure abandonment.

She laid her head against my shoulder, dragging in harsh breaths. When she finally spoke, she whispered, "One of these days, you're going to need to let me reciprocate."

I throbbed. I worried I might actually explode in my jeans. "It's not about reciprocity, sweetheart. But, if you're offering, then maybe—do you think you can come home with me? I want you in my bed."

She brought her head back up to meet my gaze. Her fingertips brushed the length of my erection, and I nearly choked. "I want to. I'm not sure I can get away with that though. It's sort of a girls' night. And my class is meeting in the morning for an early shoot."

I squeezed my eyes shut as all blood in my body flowed right out to my burning hard cock. With the last vestige of control, I nodded briskly. "Okay. But this weekend though. I want you in my bed."

She sighed softly as I readjusted her clothes. "Done, but I'm issuing my formal protest. I don't care where we are."

"I do." I forced myself away from her. "Let's go back to your friends before one of them comes looking for you."

"Fine, I'll behave."

With my hand on the door, I kissed her briefly. "I was thinking, how about instead of you just coming over, we go on an actual date. You know, where I take you to dinner, maybe a little dancing. Just us. No crew."

She grinned. "Like a grown-up date?"

"Yeah, let's pretend to be grown up for a minute." I swung her hand gently. "I want to show you off. No more sneaking off or pretending I'm not desperate to touch you." I needed Gemma to move up her timeline.

Taking Abbie's hand in mine, I opened the door. Immediately, flashbulbs blinded me. Time slowed in that moment. The flash of the bulb hadn't yet extinguished, but I yanked Abbie back into the room and slammed the door.

"Fuck! Fuck! Fuck!"

She stumbled before righting herself on the bed. "Alexi, what the hell?"

Adrenaline coursed through my veins. I dragged my hands through my hair. "Shit, Abbie, I'm sorry. I'm so fucking sorry."

Eyes wide, she blinked up at me. "For what?"

"The damn paparazzi. Shit. I fucked up."

A frown furrowed her brow. "Seriously, Alexi, what's going on? Why are you freaking out? Just tell me what—"

I couldn't even process her questions. "We need to get the hell out of here. I'm going to open the door, and I need you to shield your face. Can you take your hair down and duck your head?"

She stared up at me. "So, you're not planning to tell me what the hell is going on?"

"Abbie, I can't right now. Please, just trust me, okay? I need to get you out of here. I'll explain everything. Later." Much later. Once I'd taken care of the fucking paparazzi and could think past the buzzing in my ears. "Please, I'm begging you."

She stood smoothly. Reaching up to her hair, she removed an elastic and several pins so that the braids shielded her face. "This good enough?"

Her eyes were wide and guarded. Pain sliced through me. I was losing her. I'd freaking blown it. "Yeah." I took her hand and squeezed. "I'll take you back to Sophie and Max, and I'll take care of the arsehole with the camera."

She tugged on her hand a little, but I didn't let her go.

"Alexi, we're going to talk about this, right?"

I worked my jaw. "We will. Just not now." I had to fix this. Somehow.

CHAPTER ELEVEN

LEX

Shitstorm didn't cover the depth of the mess I found myself in. My phone rang on the nightstand, and I peeled open gritty eyes to glare at it. Five in the morning. When I saw Gemma's name, I cursed.

The moment I answered, it was clear she'd been crying. Through a round of muffled and choked tears, she whispered, "Fuck, I'm so sorry, Lex."

"Hey, hey. You didn't fuck up. I did. All of this is my fault. Unfortunately, I'm reaping what I sowed."

"No, Lex. I saw her talking to that piece of slime, and I didn't put two and two together until we left the club. I confronted her about it, and she denied it, but I don't believe her."

"What are you talking about, Gems?"

"Jacinda. She called the paparazzi. She's the one who had the photos leaked."

I sat up in bed, and my skull throbbed. "What the fuck?"

"God, I'm so sorry. I never thought she'd do something like this to force my hand."

Shit. Shit. Shit. What the hell was I supposed to do now? If the paparazzi thought they had a credible source, there was no getting in front of the story. "How bad is it?"

"It's bad, Lex. Every other minute or so, I get a new notification on my Google alerts."

I hung up with Gemma then lay back in my bed. "Fuck!" The curse came on the wing of a primal roar I swore would wake my neighbors. I'd had less than two months with Abbie before things had gone to shit.

By the time Nick called, any sliver of hope I held onto had evaporated. "Were you ever going to tell me, mate?"

I bit out a curse. "Sorry, Nick. I didn't exactly know what to say. 'Hey, I'm falling in love with some American girl.' It wasn't supposed to happen, but it did."

My friend was silent for a moment. "I don't know how you could do this to Gemma. She's a great girl."

I walked over to my dresser and grabbed a pair of sweats. Since I was up, I might as well go for a run. "Yes, she is. But to be honest, she's been more my friend than girlfriend or fiancée for a while. And she knew I was falling for Abbie."

I could picture the confused frown on Nick's face. "I don't understand. Gemma knew, and you guys didn't break up?"

I wasn't ready to go into the whole mess. Besides, I couldn't. Not without outing Gemma, and I still had to protect her as best I could. "Look, it's complicated. We've pretended to be a couple to keep our parents off our backs. But this is serious now. Toshino was clear in the indemnity clause on the contract. They wanted no negative press. If either of us steps out of line within these six months of transition they can back out of the deal. And with the paparazzi sniffing around, this puts everything at risk." I ran my hands through my hair. I needed to get a hold of Toshino. "We're fucked."

He sighed. "Look. So far, I've heard nothing, but I'm on it. And there is only press on your personal relationship. So far no one knows of the sale or interim CEO position, so if we can keep it under wraps, we're golden. I'll also try to get in front of it, if I can. I'll call the lawyer when we hang up. What's your next move?"

"Fuck, I don't know. I'm caught between dealing with Abbie or trying to get in front of my father. If he's heard, he'll be furious and try to slap some restraints on me or something. He still can't actually make me join his company, but it's going to be ugly."

"Okay, then maybe it's best you stay out of his way. I'll do what I can on my end and let you know what happens."

"Cheers, Nick."

"Uh, Lex?"

"Yeah, mate?"

"Do you really love her?"

My stomach knotted at the word love and it doubled me over. "Yes."

"Then I'm sorry this has turned into a clusterfuck. I hope she'll listen to you."

"You and me both." She probably wouldn't. But it was still early enough she might not have seen it yet. Even if she had, I had to try to explain.

My brother was the final call of the early morning. All Xander said was, "Well, at least I know I couldn't have fucked everything up this bad."

"Seriously? Alexander, I clearly don't need this shit right now." Quickly, I tugged on socks and my trainers. At least I could run out some of my frustration.

Xander was silent for a beat. "Do you think any of it will come up?"

Icicles formed in my veins. I hadn't given any thought to what would happen with a media scandal. All the Chase family secrets would come crawling out of the darkened shadows. "I don't know, Xan. I'll call the lawyer and see about a gag order."

"Let me do it." Xander sighed. "You sound like shit."

"Thanks for that."

"Well, you do. Any word from the old man yet?"

"No, but I'm sure it'll come. But something like this is beneath his concern unless he thinks it tarnishes him in some way." I sighed. "I'm not sure how I fucked this all up so badly."

"Well, that'll teach you to snatch a woman right from under your brother's nose."

I ground my teeth. "She wasn't yours, Xan."

"I know. I couldn't have her anyway. And let's face it. I'm even more of a mess than you are. If it's any consolation, I would have fucked this up even more spectacularly than you have."

My heart squeezed. "I love her, Xander."

"Then fucking fix it. If you managed to find a way to be truly happy, don't let that shit go for anything."

ABBIE

I whacked my alarm as it cheerily buzzed. Peeling the duvet back, I checked the time. Six thirty. My brain scrambled for any viable reason why I couldn't possibly go on the shoot this morning. But when I found none, I forced myself into a sitting position.

I shouldn't have gone out last night. My brain automatically went to those hushed moments in that darkened room. The moments before Alexi had started acting like a crazy person. I shivered at the memory of how he'd driven me to the edge of crazy. Even as the memory sank in, my core softened and contracted at the thought of his lips teasing me. But the following imagery of what had happened afterward was like taking an ice water bath.

He'd deposited me back in VIP, whispered something to Max about taking me out through the back when I was ready to go. Then he'd practically run out of the place with Nick in tow.

There was a faint knock at my door.

"Yeah. Come in."

"You up? It's your mother."

I frowned. "Unfortunately." I was not in the mood to deal with family hysterics so early in the morning.

Faith clomped in with her duvet wrapped around her and black bunny slippers on her feet. She plopped on my bed dramatically as she handed me the phone.

"Mom, is everything okay? Dad, the girls?"

My mother's voice was crisp and cold. "No, everything is

not all right. We sent you to school. Decided to support your foolish attempts, and this is how you repay us?"

An icy fist slowly wrapped frozen fingers around my gut. "Mom, you'll have to start from the beginning. I have no idea what you're talking about."

My mother scoffed. "I find that hard to believe. What daughter of mine gets herself in a tabloid magazine and doesn't think I'll ever notice? I mean, you can't get into a medical journal like your sister. You have to go and let it be something tawdry like *OK* magazine."

OK, magazine? Now I knew my mother was really out of it. "Mom, have you been having mimosas again? You have to be famous to get into that magazine. And I am distinctly not famous."

Faith patted my knee and then grabbed my laptop from the desk. I quickly typed a search for my name and *OK* magazine.

"Mom, I honestly have no idea what you're talking about."

"Stop lying, Abbie. And how could you do this to Easton? He loves you. Sometimes men just need to figure out what they want, and you go and do something like this to him. Something so public. Not to mention what you're doing to that poor girl."

Faith and I watched in horror as page after page of results appeared on the laptop screen. There, in full color, was a photo of me kissing Lex that first night on the rooftop. Then there was the one of us leaving Brixton Gold, and finally one of us coming out of the sex room last night, looking flustered and well sated. The headline read *Britain's*

Royal Billionaire Bachelor and His American Dalliance Break Fiancée's Heart.

Shitballs.

Faith stared at me.

My mother's voice sounded like it was coming from the other end of a very long tunnel. "Abena Nartey, are you listening to me?"

I could barely get the strangled breath out. "Y-yes, Mom."

"If you think this is how we behave, then I'm sorely disappointed. You're to come home immediately."

Surprise and annoyance edged to the surface. "You want me to *what?*"

"You heard me. Come home. This little trip down rebellion lane has lasted long enough. You'll come home, and we'll sort this out as a family."

"But there's nothing to sort out. I met a guy. We've sort of been seeing each other." I slid a look at Faith and noted the tight set of her lips. "It's not that big of a deal." Except our relationship was all over *OK* fucking magazine.

The room spun. Why were we in *OK?* Then I read the headline again. *Royal? Fiancée?* I sucked in a deep breath and tried to focus on what my mother was saying.

"Mom, I'm not coming home. Despite what you see, I'm actually thriving here. I'm getting to explore all kinds of things." *In the bedroom...* "My course is going well." *Okay, so small fibs didn't count.* "I'm working hard like you've taught me to do all my life. Is this really about the fact that I'm in a magazine, or is this about the fact that you no longer control me?"

My mother's voice went up an octave. "Control? You

think this is about control? We'll see how you feel about control when we stop paying for school."

Fuck. Sweat popped on my brow. "You would do that?"

My mother sniffed. "We would be happy to pay for you to go to a school closer to home, or for you to go to law school, or medical school, but this... This frivolous thing has thrown you off track."

Tears burned my eyes. "So you're saying that you and Dad, that would be it, you would cut me off just for doing what I think is best for me?"

"It's your choice, Abbie. But we're not going to support you making poor decisions. Leaving Easton. Running off to London. Dating this piece of cheating scum. I don't care if he is royalty. You're nothing more than someone to be used and discarded to him. At least Easton loved you."

Fury made my voice tight. "Easton hit me, Mother. He hit me. That's not love. If you actually cared about me and were less concerned with social standing, you'd see that he would have killed me eventually."

I swallowed hard, not daring to look at Faith.

"If you do not come home immediately, you are drawing the line in the sand."

Hot tears brimmed in my eyes. "I guess I have, then, because I am certainly not coming home."

My mother hung up on me.

Too shocked to move, I sat starring at my wall of photos from home. So that was it. I was completely on my own.

Faith put a hand on my knee. "You and I are going to discuss your secrecy later. Much later. Right now, you need a hug and some reinforcements."

Frozen with shock, I let her drag me into a hug. Well, I'd wanted my freedom. Now I had it.

An hour later, I was getting the third degree.

"Shit, Abbie, when were you going to tell us?" Sophie had wasted no time. She'd barged into the front door five minutes after I had gotten off the phone.

I tucked my knees under me as I looked up at Sophie and Faith, both pacing the length of our living room. "I don't know. Never maybe."

Faith stamped her foot. "If there was ever a reason to *not* keep something secret him abusing you was it. And I know you were going through stuff with Easton, but you should have told us. We never would have let you stay with him."

Sophie nodded in agreement. "I mean, we could have helped you."

"I was ashamed and afraid. I believed him when he said no one else would want me. When he said it was my fault that he lost his temper. I was beyond anybody's help. Even yours." I shook my head. "But you know what? We'll deal with my psycho ex later. I can't deal with the dark and scary right now. Can we talk about how the fuck Alexi is a Royal? He's just a guy."

Sophie looked down. "I'm sorry, sweetie. It never even occurred to me to mention it. His mother is from some deposed line of the monarchy of Nomea. You would never know, though. He keeps things pretty private and sheltered."

I stared at her. "That would have been some good information to have."

"Honestly, I didn't know myself until recently. Max dropped that tidbit on me the night of Lex's party. I didn't think it was important. How was I supposed to know you'd end up secretly dating him?" Annoyance slipped into Sophie's voice.

"I'm sorry, guys, but honestly, I can't take it today. You can yell tomorrow. Today I have to figure out what the fuck I'm going to do. And while we're on the what-the-fuck questions—he's fucking engaged?"

Sophie winced. "I had heard that was a possibility. More like a rumor. Lex and Gemma have been together forever. Most people just assumed that if they weren't already engaged, that it would only be a matter of time."

My stomach rolled. "But he told me they were just friends."

Sophie and Faith glanced at each other. Sophie's voice was soft when she finally spoke. "No, honey. They are absolutely together. Max confirmed it. I—I'm so sorry."

I was going to be sick. All over Faith's pretty hardwood floors. *No. You are a survivor. You didn't survive Easton just to have this asshole kill you. Focus.*

I shook my head. "Okay. I'll deal with it later. Right now, priority number one is what the fuck I'm going to do about school. I'm fine for the rest of the term, but if I'm to stay here, I need to come up with cash quickly."

"Obviously, you need a job," Faith squeaked, still miffed about not being included in the Lex secret.

"No shit, Faith. What do you think I've been trying to secure for the past month?"

Faith winced. "Okay, sorry. I'm sort of in uber-bitch drive at the moment. Lex, that asshole Easton. I'm going to kill him when I see him, by the way." I shook my head. "I wish you had told us."

I sighed. "I'm sorry for all of it. I thought I was doing the best thing. I'm a thousand times sorry for not telling you. But I honestly just needed time."

Sophie sashayed over and plopped down on the settee next to me. "Okay. Now that we've established that you're sorry, that you won't keep secrets from your besties anymore, and that we'll obviously get the juicy details from you later, let's work on the main issue."

I sighed. "You know anyone who wants to give me a job?"

Sophie shrugged. "I know lots of artists, darling. One of them has to be looking for a muse."

My heart sank. "I meant like a real paying job, Soph."

She nodded. "You'd be surprised. I was the muse for a fabulous painter last year, and I earned two thousand quid in three weeks."

As intriguing as that sounded, I had a feeling that being a muse might require something that made me all kinds of uncomfortable. Like *naked* uncomfortable. Besides, I needed to depend on myself. Counting on others, no matter how well intentioned, was likely a bad call. It had already gotten me in trouble with school and with my family. "It's okay. I'll figure it out."

Faith ran a hand through her hair. "Well I might be able to get you a job at the PR firm. You'll likely just need a letter of recommendation."

I wanted to hug Faith for thinking of me, but I needed to be available to do my class assignments during most daylight hours, so a day job wasn't going to work out well.

"Hello, sorry to harp, but can we get back to the larger problem of Lex and how you ended up in *OK* magazine?" Sophie interjected. "What are you going to do about him?"

My stomach rolled. *Oh yeah him. The liar.* Why the hell was I surprised that he'd hidden some key details about himself? Just like Easton.

"He lied about who he was. About who he was going to marry. About everything. I have no idea who he is. All I know is that the sex is good." Okay, not entirely true. I also knew that when I was with him, I felt truly alive. But that didn't matter now.

CHAPTER TWELVE

ABBIE

My phone rang, and I popped my head out of the covers to glare at it. Sophie brought it over for me.

"Doesn't say a name, only a number."

"What's the number?" I grumbled.

Sophie rattled off the digits, and I shook my head. "Nope, that's Alexi."

Sophie pressed ignore, then turned it off. "There that's better. Safer if you don't have to hear it ring."

Faith brought some tea over and set it down on the coffee table. "I don't know, guys. I mean, he's a first-class wanker, but perhaps she should hear him out."

Sophie scowled. "Even if she does eventually decide to take him back, she can't just talk to him right away. That looks desperate. She's going to have to make him beg for it. It's the only way he'll learn."

"Faith, I don't get it. You had such a hard line with Easton."

"That's because I know how much you gave up with

116

Easton. Don't get me wrong. I liked the guy enough when you were together, and you seemed happy with him at first, but as time wore on, you were more like a shell of yourself. And now that I know what you were going through, I shudder to think of what you were *really* going through that I didn't see." She sighed. "But with Lex, you've been bubbly these last few weeks. Happy, despite all the crazy and the stress. Granted, I thought it was your hot professor, but all I'm saying is you've been happy. When you're happy, I can be lenient."

"Yeah, well, I'm not happy anymore, am I?" I grabbed a tissue and blew my nose, then dropped the tissue in the wastebasket the girls had left by the couch for me. "I mean, I thought I was falling for this guy." I sat up, dragging the duvet around me so no part of my skin was exposed to the chilly air. "I've never felt as... combustive as I have with Alexi."

"Ah, passion. There's no real substitute for it, is there?" muttered Sophie. Her expression was contemplative. "I have to ask though, what do you really know about him besides how great he is in bed—which I want to hear all about by the way. He's been friends with Max for years, but he's really private. Beyond surface stuff, I haven't ever gotten much."

Faith frowned. "Sophie has a point. I hate to say it. I mean he's hot, and I'm sure you guys have had your, erm, moments, but in that deep connection way, have you actually talked about anything real? Did he tell you anything about himself?"

My head throbbed. I racked my brain, thinking back to our earlier conversations. We'd talked about his parents, his brother, about his dreams. But basic stuff, I didn't know—like that he had a fiancée. Or where he worked exactly. Or what he did. Or what he spent his spare time doing. He'd mentioned parental angst, but again, had never gone into detail. Instead, he'd listened to me, prodding for more information about me. Shit. Sophie was right. I was in love with the way he made me feel. *Not* with the guy.

And while I was in no mood for company, Faith and Sophie insisted. Granted, when Sophie had tried to pop out to the corner shop, she'd been met by a hoard of paparazzi on the front steps. They both declared that I needed to stay somewhere calm until the storm blew over.

In just over an hour they had me safely ensconced in Max's house, far away from the ringing home line and the buzzing of the door. Sophie had gone on a full reconnaissance mission, scouting down the street to make sure Lex wasn't lurking, waiting to try to talk to me. I had tried to tell them he wouldn't bother, but neither one listened as they shuffled me through the back door and into Sophie's car.

Now as I sat huddled between Faith and Jasper, I watched the parade of model-boys flit around the house in various stages of undress. Now I understood why Sophie was never in our flat. Hell, *I* never wanted to leave this magical land of hot men.

All the guys, Jasper especially, were surprisingly sweet. Oh, he still flirted, but he toned down his more outrageous tendencies. Though his flirting made me feel somewhat normal.

Max was the consummate host. Told me to think of the house as mine. Whatever I needed, all I had to do was ask. I felt like I'd been enveloped into a large rag-tag family. There were two new models renting rooms as well. Even though they didn't know me, they went out of their way to make me comfortable.

When Jasper headed out that night, he told me to take his room as he wouldn't be back till the morning.

"Oh, no, I couldn't. The couch is fine."

He laughed. "Look, the sheets are clean, and it makes me smile thinking of you in my bed."

I just rolled my eyes. *Shameless.* "No really."

"I insist. You can sleep on the couch if you want, but honestly, the bed is more comfortable."

"Okay, I'll think about it."

Sophie took Jasper's spot, flanking me. "Honestly, Abbie, don't beat yourself up over this. How were you supposed to know all this?"

"And he did like you. *Does*, like you," Faith amended quickly.

"I'm not so sure about that. I just want to forget I ever met him. You see what they're saying in the papers. That I broke up him and Gemma. That *I'm* the other woman. *He* did that to me. Humiliated me in public."

Sophie nodded sympathetically. Faith nodded too, but her expression held a note of reservation.

"I still need to figure out what I'm going to do about a job. I've been searching the campus job listings, and still nothing. I'm going to need to take it off campus. Problem is, no part-time job will really do the trick."

Angel trotted down the stairs. With his deeply tanned skin, sandy brown hair, bright green eyes, and killer angular face, not to mention ripped, shirtless body, I had no problem seeing why he was a model. There would probably be millions of women willing to pay to have him walk around their houses in various stages of undress.

When he spoke, his voice was heavily accented. He sounded Middle Eastern, maybe Israeli. "You're a photographer, right?"

I nodded slowly. "Yeah."

"Well, I need some of my headshots redone, as I'm looking for a new agency. Would you think about doing them?"

I smiled. Taking some pictures might help keep my mind occupied. "Yeah, sure. When do you need them by?"

"End of next week would be great. I could pay you two hundred pounds. I'd planned to shell out a lot more for them, so now it's a win-win."

I perked up. "Wait, you'd be paying me?"

He grinned, and I was so temporarily blinded by his sheer beauty that I could only stare, slack-jawed.

"Well, yeah. Didn't you just say you needed a job?"

"Yes, but—"

"Max said to give you whatever you wanted. You want a job, you have one. I'll check with some of the other models I know. Some actors too. Everyone needs a good photographer."

I blinked at him. "How do you know I'm any good?"

He nodded toward Sophie. "Sophie brought home that one you'd taken in Brixton with the kids krumping. It's pretty killer." He shrugged. "Besides, it's good karma to help out a beautiful girl. Just tell me anything else you need, and it's yours." His smile was just this side of interested and super sexy as he headed into the kitchen.

Something told me he was offering me more than just a job. But unfortunately, he didn't do it for me. It didn't matter how pretty he was.

After he vanished down the back stairs to the kitchen, Faith and I stared agog at Sophie.

"Did he just offer to sleep with you to make you feel better?" Faith squeaked.

I stared after him. "I'm not sure."

Sophie shrugged. "Couldn't hurt. Best way to get over someone, and all that."

I shook my head. "Just what has Max told these guys to do for me?"

"Oh, I don't think that had anything to do with Max, babes. I think he genuinely wants your body."

Oh. Well, then. "As pretty as he is to look at, I'm staying away from uber-hot guys for a while. It's probably safer that way."

ABBIE

Under the cover of night and away from Sophie's judging eyes, I climbed into bed with my phone. The good news was, I had a paying gig lined up. A decent paying gig. I just needed more of those.

Max had gotten two new models in the house that night so the spare room I'd been sleeping in was occupied. I'd taken

Jasper up on his offer and was frankly glad I did. His bed was soft, and the electric blanket chased the chill away.

The bad news was that I still had to face the outside world come morning. I couldn't very well ignore my assignment, which meant I'd have to head out into Soho tomorrow to capture street fashion. Maybe I could convince Sophie to go with me. Faith had to work. I could always ask Angel or somebody to tag along with us for the day and grab some shots of him, but when they weren't working, the boys tended toward sloppy hipster chic with skinny jeans and faded ironic T-shirts. But it wouldn't hurt to ask. They also knew a load of female models, so that could make my assignment pretty easy.

With a deep breath and a silent prayer, I sat up under the blanket and turned on both of my phones. As I waited for the screens to light up, my breathing and my heart rate increased. Both phones immediately started to vibrate. *Shit.* Between the two, there were eleven missed calls and fifteen texts. My hands shook as I checked the voicemails first.

Alexi.

"Jesus, shit. Abbie, I'm so sorry. I—"

I deleted it without listening to the rest of the message.

The next was from my sister Akos. "Fuck, Abbie, what kind of mess have you gotten yourself into? I mean of all the moronic—"

I deleted that one too.

The next one was from Ilani. "Oh, you dark horse, you. Look, I know it's probably messy and all right now, but if you need to chat, I'm here. Call me."

My shoulders slumped. It was sweet of Ilani to call, but I

wasn't in the mood to deal with anyone. I'd just have to wait and see her at school.

The rest of the messages included one from my mother telling me she'd already pulled the funds for my second semester out of my bank account and stating her disappointment. Silence from my father. *So much for him admiring me.* Two more from my sisters, and one from Easton, insisting that I call him right away.

Right. On to the texts.

I squeezed my eyes shut when my screen lit up, slowly opening one lid at a time. Alexi, Alexi... They were all from Alexi.

"I'm sorry."

"Please let me explain."

"Please don't shut me out."

"I'm coming over."

They were all a variation of the I-know-I-fucked-up-please-believe-me theme.

But I wasn't going to do that any time soon. I couldn't deal with him right now. Couldn't deal with any of it. It wasn't so much that he hadn't told me who he was. But more about the way he'd gone about it. He'd had a million opportunities. He'd slept with me knowing he was deceiving me. Knowing I had no idea. I'd slept with a total stranger. One who had more secrets than anyone I'd ever met.

Tears stung my eyes as I deleted all his text messages. How had I gotten it so wrong? He'd said he cared about me, but that wasn't how you showed someone you cared. I'd fabricated all of that in my mind. I'd need time before I could deal with him.

I eventually drifted into a fitful sleep. Tossing and turning, wishing that Alexi would call, then wishing he wouldn't.

It was three in the morning when I heard Jasper and Max finally stumble home. They weren't being too loud, but since I was up, I heard every footstep.

When Jasper opened the door to his room, I immediately sat up. "Hey. I'm sorry. You said I could sleep here so..." I cleared my throat. "Faith stayed the night, so she's on the couch."

Jasper just blinked at me like a kid on Christmas morning who couldn't quite believe he'd gotten the gift he'd asked for. "Ahh, that would explain why the bundle on the couch didn't slap me when I suggested I might snuggle in."

He laughed when I rolled my eyes.

"It's cool. I like you in here. Now my sheets are going to smell like you."

Oh Jasper, always outrageous. I hated the weakness that made me consider staying, and I didn't want to be alone, so I hesitated but finally said, "I'll grab a duvet and head to the media room to sleep on one of the recliners."

Jasper halted me with a hand on my foot. "No, don't."

"But I'm in your bed. Where are you going to sleep?"

He grinned, and I stammered. "O-oh, no, I don't think that will work."

"Look, we'll just sleep, okay? I can be a friend." He smiled sheepishly. "Besides, I'm knackered. And you look like you could use a friend."

I chewed my bottom lip. I didn't particularly want to be alone, but I didn't want to give him the wrong impression either. "Just friends. And you'll keep your hands to yourself?"

Jasper put his hand over his heart. "I swear to be on my best behavior."

I nodded.

After changing in the bathroom, he slid into the bed next to me. If I closed my eyes and snuggled into the cocoon of his warmth, I could pretend he was Alexi. Just to help me sleep...

Jasper kissed my shoulder and wrapped an arm around my waist, tugging me close to his body. Just as my eyes fluttered closed, he whispered, "But if you did want me to go down on you or something, I promise I'm willing and very good. I like to take my time with a woman's body. You can pretend I'm anyone you want."

I swatted the arm around me. "Hands off, Jas, or I'm sleeping on the living room floor."

With a sigh, he rolled away. "Okay. Fair enough." His hand twitched against mine. "How about your hand? Can I hold your hand?"

I rolled on my back to match his position and stared at the ceiling even as a tear rolled down my face. "Yeah, that would be great."

When he took my hand, his was firm and warm and comforting. And he was kind enough not to say anything about the sound of my tears in the silence.

CHAPTER THIRTEEN

LEX

The following morning, my head throbbed as Jasper, Angel, Nick, and Max all convened on the barge. I hadn't gotten a wink of sleep, and I wasn't in the mood for the mental beat down I was about to endure. And to make matters worse, Abbie hadn't replied to a single one of my messages.

"Mate, what the fuck were you thinking?"

I glared at Max. I really didn't need my friend taking the moral high ground with me. "Look, it wasn't supposed to happen like that. The whole thing just got fucking messy, okay?"

"She's a nice girl. You really should have left her alone." Jasper's voice was barely above a snarl.

"And what, left her for you?" I growled.

"Maybe." Jasper stood to glare at me.

Nick stepped between the two of us. "Come on, you two. Are you really going to get in a row over some bird? Use your brains." He turned his attention to Angel and Max. "A little help here?"

Angel shook his head. "I was just looking for a lift to the agency. I'm starting to think I should have taken the tube."

Max shrugged. "I didn't think I'd agree with Nick on this one, but he's right. We've been mates for how long? Stop being mad for just a moment and use the brains God gave ya."

I dragged in a breath. "I just want to know that she's okay."

"She's fine," Max said. "Well, as fine as she can be. Sophie's got her holed up at the house, and she and Faith are pretty much circling her like mother hens."

I breathed a sigh of relief. I hadn't been able to reach her, which was to be expected, but I was worried that she wasn't okay. And when I'd seen the paparazzi camped on her lawn, I'd really worried. "Okay good. At least she's not all alone in her flat with the vultures circling."

"Would there be any vultures if it weren't for you?" Jasper grumbled.

"No, I'll admit, I cocked this whole thing up. But there were some extenuating circumstances I couldn't avoid."

"Oh, you mean like already having a fiancée?" Jasper made to stand again, but Nick shoved him back into his seat.

"Easy, both of you. Jas has a point though. What about Gem? Have you seen her, talked to her?"

Gemma was staying out of sight at Jacinda's. She'd stayed with me a couple of nights, but then the press had gotten so ridiculous she'd needed to escape. "I talked to her this morning. She's fine."

Nick frowned. "What do you mean fine?"

"I mean *fine*." What the hell could I tell them? That Gemma had seen it coming? That she'd apologized to me profusely again because she suspected Jacinda had gotten pissed enough about Gemma's closeted status to call the press and force her hand? That my relationship with Gem had been a sham? I was sick of this shit. But I couldn't really tell them with Angel there. "Look, Gemma and I have some logistics to work out, but we haven't really been intimate for a long time."

"I know that's what you said before. But why stay with her?" Nick asked, his brows furrowing.

I swiped my hair off my forehead. Habit sounded too callous, but it was the truth. Gemma probably hadn't needed me to shield her for nearly so long, but I'd done it because I had no one in my life that I wanted to be single for. "It's complicated."

Nick shook his head. "You lot are a pair. When I talked to her this morning, she seemed more concerned about you and how you were handling things with the press than she did about your relationship."

I nodded. "See, there you go, she's fine." I turned my attention to Angel, Max, and Jasper. "Now come on, do me a solid. I need to speak with Abbie, if I can."

Max merely shook his head while Jasper muttered, "Fuck no. I look like a better option if you remain a fuck up. To the victor go the spoils and all that."

Max slid a narrowed glance at his flat mate. "Jas, for once, give it a rest. He's clearly already shattered." Max turned his attention back to me. "Look, no can do. Sophie will kill me, and honestly Abbie looks like she needs a break. Maybe when she's more settled."

I scrubbed my face with my hands. How the hell was I going to fix this if I couldn't even talk to her?

CHAPTER FOURTEEN

LEX

"Lex, I'm so sorry. I didn't intend for this to happen."

I shifted uncomfortably on the park bench. When Gemma had asked me to meet her in Hyde Park, I'd been a little dubious, considering Jacinda and her penchant for calling paparazzi. "Gem, I know it's not your fault. You wouldn't have ever done something like this. You're not responsible for her actions."

"But you got hurt because I couldn't be an adult and accept some things about who I am, so I feel terrible."

I shook my head. "Still not your fault. She retaliated and that was uncalled for. Especially the way she did it." I shoved my hands into my pockets to ward off some of the cold. "Look, I'm not telling you who to be with, but you should be with someone who doesn't try to manipulate you into the outcome they want."

She rubbed her nose. "Yeah, I know."

"You're far too smart for that, and you deserve better."

"You know, you're probably the safest, healthiest relationship I've ever had."

Laughter bubbled up from my chest. "Then aren't we a pair, because we are royally fucked up. This whole thing is fucked up." I shook my head. "I thought I was doing you this favor, but I probably did more damage in the long run. As for me, I was just hiding from a real relationship. I'm as fucked up as Xander is with his string of women."

She wrinkled her nose. "You're nothing like Xander."

A cold fist of ice wrapped around my gut. After the hell we'd gone through as kids, neither one of us had ever learned to fully trust anyone. And God knew how fucked up our love lives were. What would she think if she realized I was more like Xander than I could ever admit? Worse, what would Abbie say? "He's my brother. He's part of me and vice versa."

"I wish you wouldn't say that. You go through life separate from people, and you're secretive. You act like no one could ever love you, and I just hope you find someone who can, because you deserve it."

I swallowed around the lump in my throat. *I want Abbie.* Yeah, well, no amount of wanting her was going to make her manifest in front of me. She was my only chance at a real human connection in the last five years, and I'd fucked it up. "Maybe one day."

"I still think you should let me talk to her."

"No dice, Gemma. It was my fuck up. You don't have to clean up my mess for me."

She narrowed her eyes. "You mean like you've been cleaning up my messes for me? Without you, I might not have survived the last five years, and I'm well aware of it. You've been my rock, and you've kept me sane and made me feel loved. It's the least I can do."

"And I said no."

She pursed her lips and turned to face the lawn. I knew that look; she was stewing. But let her stew. Abbie wanted to be left alone; I wouldn't have my life intrude on hers. I cleared my throat. "So, I guess we should officially do this then."

She sniffled. "Yeah, it's about that time."

I took her hand out of habit, like I always did when I wanted to tell her something serious. "Gemma, I love you, but it's time for us to break up."

CHAPTER FIFTEEN

ABBIE

It had been exactly three days, nine hours, and fifty-seven minutes since my London life imploded. And now I had to deal with this shit. I scowled at the brunette beauty in the foyer. When Jasper had told me someone had come to see me, I'd expected Ilani. Not Gemma.

"If you're here to shiv me, I think Lex already beat you to the punch."

Gemma glanced around. "I've never actually been back here before. Max has tons of parties, but I never managed to accompany Lex to one."

I stood and raised an eyebrow. "Are we going to talk home and gardens, or are you going to tell me what you're doing out here? I know South London is a bit out of the way from posh Mayfair, or wherever it is you live."

Gemma blew out a breath. "I'm not here to bother you, I swear."

"Then you're failing, because I'm bothered. I don't want to listen to any more apologies from him. I'm done with listening to his voicemails and reading his emails and his personally delivered messages. There's nothing he can say to make me forget what he did to me, humiliating me like that."

Gemma blew out a breath then rocked back on her heels. "I'm actually to blame for it all. This had nothing to do with Lex."

"I'm not sure what you're talking about, but I don't—I can't..." I tried again and reined my emotions in. My heart screamed that I needed to listen to Gemma, but my brain silenced the voice of dissent. "You and him and your screwed-up relationship is none of my business. Now if you'll excuse me, I need to go before more of your paparazzo friends see us talking and decide to splash me on some more magazines."

"Look, I wasn't followed. I just wanted to talk to you for a minute."

I crossed my arms. "Your minute is ticking."

"Wow, you're tough. I can see why he likes you."

I didn't need Alexi's fiancée patronizing me. "You've got forty-five seconds."

"I'm a lesbian."

I shook my head to make sure I heard correctly. "Excuse me?"

"I'm a lesbian."

I still wasn't sure I'd heard her correctly. "Wow, I'm not an expert in coming out, but I get the impression this is a very awkward version of it."

Gemma chuckled. "It's the first time I've said it out loud since I first told Lex."

What the hell was I supposed to say? There was no

follow up to that, except, *uh, okay.* "I'm not sure why I need to know this."

"It's important because, back in Uni, Lex agreed to be my sometimes boyfriend to keep my parents off my back. At first, it was just this thing we did when we were out. Then it was like we were really going out, except for all the sex stuff. He has been protecting me for years. Keeping my secret."

"This can't be real."

"It's the truth, Abbie. My parents will disown me when I tell them, and I was terrified of being left without family or a support system, or I would have cut him loose years ago. The truth is I used him. I knew I was being unfair and did it anyway. I needed him. I didn't care that he only had these half relationships with women, that he never got close to anyone. I suspect there's a reason he never wanted a real relationship, but he's never told me what it is."

Sucking in shaky breath, I said, "I'm still not sure what I'm supposed to do with this information."

"I don't know, go be with him. However this is supposed to end in the romantic comedy. Girl gets the guy."

"Look, Gemma, I appreciate you coming to talk to me, but that doesn't change anything. He still lied to me."

"Only to protect me. He didn't want to betray my trust."

"I know you see it that way, but he still lied. He never had to betray your trust. All he had to say was 'I have a fiancée.' It was that simple. But he never said that. Not once. That's why I'm still angry. Then he put me in the situation to get caught and have the paparazzi on my ass twenty-four-seven."

"I concede that he might have lied, but he had a good reason. I'm really sorry you got caught in the crosshairs."

Gemma turned to leave but halted, and her smile was sad. "He's my crutch. I secretly hoped one day I could love him the way I should. As if I could grow those feelings like a fungus. I wanted to love him. I just couldn't."

"Apparently controlling the heart isn't an easy task," I muttered.

⚜

ABBIE

By day seven of the media frenzy, I was ready to climb the walls. I couldn't stay hidden anymore, and I had an assignment to complete. Besides, I also had a meeting with a graphics company who wanted to use some of my photos, and I couldn't ignore potential income just because of a broken heart... or a hoard of paparazzi on the front steps.

As I packed my camera bags, Sophie came in with her sad-and-concerned face plastered on. "Abbie, the press is still all over the flat and probably at your school. I don't think it's a good idea for you to be running around on your own."

I rolled my eyes. "Look, I know. I'm fine. I'm going to wear a disguise while I'm out and about. But I'm in need of some serious alone time. You guys have been great and more gracious than I deserve, but honestly, it's time."

I held up the paper boy hat, sunglasses, and orange and red scarf. "Besides working will keep my mind off of things. And I want to do some more research on Xander's past work. I want to get a better understanding of what he's looking for from us when he gives us assignments. I don't plan to ever fail again, so as much as I appreciate the concern, I don't have time for another 'are you really okay' conversation."

Sophie raised her eyebrows. "Fine, but I wasn't going to ask you if you were okay."

I cocked my head. "So then why did you come in here with the creased brow, worried eyes, and chewing on your bottom lip?"

Sophie laughed. "Okay, a little concerned."

"And like I said, I'm fine. Well not exactly fine, but I'll get there. Working will help." I dragged on my olive-green coat with the high collar. The paps might be out and about, but they'd have a hell of a time getting an easy shot of me.

Sophie frowned again. "Listen. I didn't want to say anything in front of Faith, but about Lex, I think you should know—"

I huffed out a breath. "Know what, that he's an asshole? Check. That he's a liar? Check. That I need to stay very far away from him? I promise you that's the plan."

Sophie chewed her lip again, then her features smoothed out. "You're right. You're a big girl." She grabbed the kettle and started prepping tea. "Speaking of being a big girl, I heard Jasper come in late last night or rather early this morning. Where did he sleep?"

My skin went hot and prickly. "Uh, he slept in his bed. *Just* slept."

Sophie grinned. "Uh-huh. You know that poor man has a serious crush on you."

Oh, I knew. Especially after last night, I knew. "You're ridiculous. Nothing happened."

"If you say so."

I laughed and slung my bag over my shoulder. The familiar weight of my equipment soothed me. Maybe, just maybe, the dark gray clouds of the whole week would start to lift.

I left Camberwell and hopped the bus to the West End. After several hours of pounding the pavement in Covent Garden and hitting up Oxford Street, somehow managing to refrain from buying anything, I hopped on the tube to school. No one seemed to recognize me. There was the occasional odd look in my direction, but given my complete stealth attire, they probably thought I was one of the East End actresses or something. Some schoolboy actually came up to me and asked if I'd been on the telly. Maybe I should opt for the undercover look more often. For all my covert movements, there wasn't a single pap in sight. Maybe they'd finally gotten bored.

Once I got to campus, the tension rolled out of my shoulders. There, nobody would give a shit who I was. Everyone was too busy working or studying to care. I rounded the building for the photography labs and froze.

"You know, you're a very hard woman to get a hold of," Alexi said as he pushed himself up from the stairs of the lab.

I tamped down the joy that bubbled in my chest at the sight of him. Instead, I nurtured cold fury. "I don't have time to talk to you right now, Alexi."

"Abbie, please. Look, I know I fucked up, but *please* hear me out."

I whirled on him. "Just what exactly am I supposed to hear out? The part about how you completely lied about who you were? Or how about the part where you had a freaking fiancée? Or maybe the part about when you said you cared about me and kept lying to me?"

A few students milled about and darted glances in our direction, so I snapped my jaw shut. Picking up my pace, I nearly ran for the printing lab.

He followed on my heels. "Look, it wasn't like that. I really fell for you."

"Oh, really? Then when the hell were you going to tell me who you were?"

His lips flattened. "Abbie, I was going to tell you. I just liked the idea of you not knowing who I was. I liked being normal with you."

"Okay, then, how about this question. Just when were you planning on actually breaking up with Gemma?"

Again silence.

"It's complicated, Abbie."

"I'm not sure what you're here to discuss, Lex," I said as I unlocked the door to the photo lab and the familiar smell of chemicals assailed me. I froze when I dropped my bag on the light table. It was difficult not to remember our first time in there, clawing at each other. Unable to keep our hands off one another.

"I should have told you." His voice was soft, pained, and a little hoarse. "I opened my mouth a dozen times to tell you. But when I met you, you didn't seem to have any idea who I was, and I liked that. To you, I was just some bloke you met on the street. I really wanted you to like me for me."

I whirled on him. "I did like you. But that's because I thought I was dealing with a real person. You're not real. You're this shinier version of the guy I was starting to fall for."

He winced, but that didn't stop me. All the anger and frustration and sadness from the last week bubbled up to the surface. "I don't know anything about you. Though I suppose if I want to learn, I could just look it up on the Internet."

"Abbie, I'm so sorry. I never intended for anything like this to happen." He shoved his hands into his pockets.

"I'm a private person, Lex. I don't need people poking around in my life. Do you know that the paparazzi were camped on my doorstep, waiting to ambush me? If it hadn't been for Faith and Sophie, I'd still be a prisoner in my house."

"I didn't know I had paparazzi on my tail until you pulled back from that kiss. Then I saw him in the shadows, and I saw the flash of his camera."

My whole body deflated, and my shoulders sagged. "That's why you got us out of there?"

He shoved his hand through his hair. "Yes. I didn't want all that shit following us around. From the moment I rescued you from that car, I felt completely connected to you. I couldn't believe my luck when you walked into my party. Then you started to talk to me. You were smart, and funny, and you had no idea who I was. You just thought I was me. I didn't want who I was to break us. I have never been happier than that weekend we spent at your place. And the week after."

I straightened my back, even though I could feel my heart melting. "That still doesn't account for the fact that I know nothing about you. But you know everything about me. You know what I'm afraid of? You know why I ran away from home, and you know what my dreams are. You won't, or can't, tell me any of those things about yourself."

"I want to, Abbie. I want to. It's just complicated. I can't tell you everything."

Even as my heart warmed, the tiny fissures started to tear again. He still wasn't going to come clean. "Then we don't have anything to talk about."

"Abbie, all I'm asking from you is to cut me a little slack." He sighed and let his head hang. "Gemma is not my fiancée, obviously. At least not in the traditional sense of the word. We've been tossed together so often, but we're no more than friends really."

I sighed. "She came to see me yesterday. She told me she's a lesbian. Is that the truth?"

He shifted from foot to foot and looked like he wasn't going to tell me, but then he pinched the bridge of his nose and started talking. "Gemma *is* a lesbian. I'm not sure if you noticed the blonde that was at my party, then at the club that night. She's Gemma's girlfriend, Jacinda."

Hope bloomed quickly, rooting in my heart and refusing to let go. "She's seriously gay?"

He sighed. "Yes. We've been pretending to be together for years. Mostly for appearances and her parents. When they find out the truth, they'll cut her off."

"So you lied for her."

He leveled a gaze at me. "Yes."

A million questions swirled in my mind, forming a tornado that threatened to short out my brain. "Wait, what happens when you want to date someone?"

"I never met anyone I wanted to be with until I met you. Until you, I've had a fling or two, but mostly just a series of meaningless encounters."

"And she just dates who she wants?"

"It's all a little complicated, but yeah. Her father is a conservative arse. When he's home, she stays with me or at a hotel. Most of the women she dates aren't out of the closet yet. Or because of their careers, they need to keep things private. Jacinda is different. She's out and wants Gemma to be too."

Too tired to think, I sat down in one of the folding chairs by the printer. "She dates, and you don't?"

"Honestly, it wasn't a problem until recently. I could just float along. When I met you, my relationship with her started to feel like a noose. I didn't want to do it anymore."

"I wish you would have told me."

"At the time, it wasn't my secret to tell. I didn't know how much trouble I was in with you until it was too late. I thought I could keep you at arm's length. But I couldn't. And I still had to protect her, but I didn't want to lose you."

"You were so busy protecting Gemma you forgot to protect me."

"Abbie, I was trying to protect you. I did everything I could do to find that photographer. You're right. I have no idea how to love someone. I honestly didn't think I was capable until that night on the roof. I wish I could fix this."

I had to steel my heart against his words. Otherwise, I'd fall back into his arms. "You can't fix it, Alexi. I have to fix my own life. Do you know my parents refuse to pay for school now?"

He paled, his normally tan skin going ashen. "Fuck. I'm so sorry, Abbie. Look it's my fault, I can—"

Furious, I pointed a finger at him. "Don't you dare offer

to pay my way. I can do this on my own. I can just see the headlines now. *Billionaire Sugar Daddy.*"

He strode over to me, his mouth tight and his dark eyes intense as he kneeled at my feet. "I'm not a billionaire. At least not yet. Not until I come into my trust fund. None of it matters if I don't have you, anyway. I don't want to lose you."

"I don't know where we go from here." Exhausted, I slumped against the printer.

From his kneeling position, he pulled me into him, wrapping his arms around my rigid frame. "I want you in my life. I..." He inhaled deeply. "I *need* you in my life."

He smelled so good. Minty and clean and fresh. It made me think of waking up in his arms with him nuzzling my neck. Like I'd found someone to love me and see me for *me.* "You can't just say the words, Lex. I need you to be open with me."

He pulled back slightly and met my gaze. "I promise. I'll tie everything up. I can give you what you need. Just please give me a chance to not fuck up."

It would be so easy to fall into him again, to just let him take care of me. But I wanted to stand on my own. I was falling for him, but after everything I'd been through, I wasn't sure if I could trust the feelings. "I... I'm not sure."

"Look, why don't we go out on Friday? I'll pick you up. You can ask me anything you want then. I'll give you the complete truth."

I met his gaze. At the end of the day, I wanted him in a way I'd never wanted Easton. I craved him. But I would walk away if I had to. I wasn't going to be that naive girl again.

"Just say yes." He kissed my hands and held them tight. "I promise, I will not fuck this up. Just believe in me."

And just like that, my heart broke in two. "Okay. Dinner. Then we'll see."

"I'll take it."

CHAPTER SIXTEEN

ABBIE

At least things on the job front were looking up. I was able to get Angel's photos taken. Then Jasper asked me to take some promotional photos of him for DJing gigs. He was willing to pay me a thousand pounds.

I was on the verge of refusing, because I didn't want charity gigs. But then I'd found out Xander charged ten thousand pounds for such work. Shoot, hadn't Julia Roberts been offered less in *Pretty Woman*?

Angel also recommended me to some of the new models in his agency. Max had come through, asking me to take real estate photos of some of his recently rehabbed houses that were up for sale.

But as loving as the model house was, I longed for the peace and relative quiet of Chiswick, so on Friday morning, I grabbed the rest of my things and headed back. By the time I got a ride back home and skirted the paparazzi hoard in front of the flat, I only had an hour and a half to get ready.

Luckily, Faith was there at the ready. "Your bathwater's

been drawn, and I picked out the top four date outfits with shoes and jewelry. Your perfumes have been narrowed down to two, and I made you something to eat, just in case you get preoccupied and don't get to dinner right away."

I stared at her perfectly organized bed with the clothes, shoes, and jewelry spread out. "How did you have time to do all this? Why did you do all this?"

Faith's eyes watered. "I told Liam I snogged Angel, and he dumped me."

"Oh, shit, wait. When did you kiss Angel?"

"A couple of nights ago when you stayed in Jasper's bed. We were up late and it just sort of happened. I told Liam, and he dumped me."

"Faith, I'm sorry." How had I missed my friend was hurting? *Because you've been a self-involved little brat.* "I've been a totally shit friend. I had no idea you were going through this. I should have been there."

Faith shook her head. "No. I only told him today. I've been feeling rotten about it. I'm not sure why I even did it. Except that Angel was beautiful. And there. And so saucy. I just wondered what it would be like. Anyway. I'm not really ready to talk about it. Still too raw, so I kept myself busy today. I skived off work and decided to help you get ready."

"Faith, I can't possibly go now. You n—"

"If you even think about backing out, I will disown you, and you'll be forced to move into the model house. And let's face it, as pretty as they are, you know that world isn't real. They are transient. You are *going* on this date. I've been waiting for a week for you to go on this date. Please let me live vicariously."

An hour and fifteen minutes later, I tried not to fidget as Faith did up the straps on the slinky sandals.

"There, stand up, let me look at you," Faith said as she stood back and stared.

I rose and went over to the mirror. "Wow." Faith had pinned back my braids in the front, giving me a swoop bang, but had let the back go wild and free and tumble down my back. It did a great job of showcasing my eyes. My brown skin seemed to shimmer at all the highlight points: my cheekbones, forehead, chin. The dramatic cat eyes made me look like a movie star. Faith had gone for a neutral matte lipstick.

"Now listen, Abbie, the lipstick will hold. I layered and mixed the shades together, so no matter what you eat or drink it should stay put. But if you start making out, you'll have to reapply. Those false lashes should also stay put at least three days, so when you wake up in his bed, you'll still have a good smoky eye look going on. I also packed make up remover towelettes in your bag as well as a couple of condoms for the night."

"Faith!" I gave her a sharp look. "I will not be sleeping with him."

Faith raised an eyebrow. "Let's face it, honey. We are all capable of doing things we say we don't want to or would never do. Just be prepared. Besides, he'll answer all your questions tonight. It'll finally be like it was meant to be, with you guys all loved up and happy."

I dropped my gaze. "I meant to say this earlier, but I never properly said it. Thanks for all of this. Thank you for not judging me, not berating me for lying and stuff. Just thanks for the overall support. I appreciate it. You've been more like family to me than my own, and I wouldn't have made it here without you. Tomorrow, you and I are going to have a good and proper sit down and talk about your situation with Liam and what the hell went wrong there. Okay?"

Faith gave me a sad smile, and her eyes shimmered, but she nodded. "Yeah, okay. Just as long as you promise that you won't skip over any of the good parts with Lex."

"Done." I seriously doubted there would be any good parts, but I wasn't telling Faith that. My friend had gone out of her way to have me look like a million dollars, including busting open a dress she hadn't worn. Faith deserved to believe in the fairytale that life had momentarily become. I'd burst that bubble tomorrow.

I did one more twirl in the mirror, enjoying the feel of the soft jersey material of the backless silver dress. It really was beautiful. From the front, the classic scoop neckline was more demure, but the back was the daring portion, being completely backless. The material started again just before the top of my ass. If I moved wrong, there'd be crack for the whole world to see.

The door buzzed, and my lungs froze. I didn't remember to breathe again until Faith jumped up.

"I'll get it. You should make an entrance."

I waited thirty seconds before going out to meet him. When he caught sight of me, Alexi stared then he swallowed, and I watched his Adam's apple bob up and down.

"You look beautiful."

My skin flushed. I bit my tongue and murmured, "Thank you. Let me get my jacket and purse."

When I trotted into the living area, Faith fanned herself.

"Wow. That man knows how to clean up. Hell, even scruffy, he's pretty. Don't forget... tomorrow, I get to live vicariously."

I grinned. "Okay, okay. You're sure I look all right?"

"You're perfect."

We bumped fists, and I tried for nonchalance as I went back into the foyer. "You ready?"

Lex nodded slowly then helped me put my coat on. "I hope you told Faith not to wait up. I have a full night planned."

"Oh, do you now?" I smirked.

He squeezed his eyes shut and shook his head. "That's not what I meant. I actually have a long date planned."

"Sorry. I couldn't resist teasing."

He grinned. "Oh, don't be. I also have high hopes."

"So where are we going?"

"Well, I promised you a proper date out on the town, so that's what we're going to do. I've taken some precautions so we don't have to deal with the paparazzi tonight, but just be aware anywhere that's not private will be open season, so you'll have to wait to jump my bones until later when we're alone."

"You're incorrigible, you know that?"

"It's the oddest thing. I feel like I've been told that before."

I chewed the inside of my cheek as I thought about the one thing that could ruin my night. I didn't want to spoil the evening before we even got started, but I needed to know what I'd have to face tomorrow. "Will it cause problems for Gemma? I know they've been pretty relentless with her too, the newshounds."

I had seen the coverage on Sky One as the paparazzi had dogged Gemma coming out of the gym, asking what she thought of her boyfriend's new paramour. She'd been more gracious than she had to be, stating that she didn't own Mr. Chase, and who he chose to spend time with was none of her business.

"Gemma's okay. She actually encouraged me to do this right and not take you to some pub. Not that I would have. But she said every woman deserves to be treated like a princess."

"She's nicer than I gave her credit for." I tucked a braid behind my ear.

"Yeah, Gem's great. There's a reason we've been friends for years. But she's not the woman I'm into. Tonight, all my focus is on you and making you comfortable."

I nodded. "Sorry. Just one more question, and we can let this go."

"It's okay, Abbie. Tonight, I have no secrets from you." He took me through the back door that led into the garden. Through there, we escaped though the opposite garage into the neighbor's driveway. Faith had already spoken to them about starting to park her car there for the time being.

Lex led me out to the waiting silver BMW sports car and opened my door. I slid in and once again couldn't get used to the plush interior. The soft leather immediately enveloped me in warmth. He'd heated the seats for me. I hated to admit it, but I knew I could get used to that kind of treatment.

"So, what happens with Gemma now?"

The engine purred, and he bypassed all the paparazzi with a small smile as he merged smoothly onto the M1. I tried not to look out the window at the cars whizzing past. He drove like a demon from hell, but also in a controlled manner that said he knew exactly what he was doing.

"It will likely be in the papers either tomorrow or the next day that she's come out as a lesbian. She's telling her family tonight."

I winced. "I feel like the catalyst that pushed her into this. No one should have to do something like that until they're ready."

"It's not your fault, Abbie. She knew this day was coming eventually. She and Jacinda have been getting closer, and Jacinda is out and proud. She wants a full-on relationship. Plus, Gem and I have acted as each other's crutches for so long it was time to sever that. Neither one of us could live a full life while we depended on the other like we did. She's stronger than she thinks. And even if her parents won't stand by her, she has me. As a friend, of course."

"Of course. And what about you? I'm sure your parents were counting on an Alexi and Gemma union."

"Well, I've been telling the old man for years that I wasn't going to marry her. He just chose not to listen. My mother, on the other hand, knew something was off. I think she thought I was the one in the closet. She's always asking me if I have passion in my life. It's really awkward."

I covered my mouth with my hand. "Oh no. She doesn't."

"She stopped asking the day we hung out in Brixton. She knew I'd met someone. I tell you she has a sixth sense about these things. She stopped thinking I was gay as soon as the pictures came out."

I blushed. "I'm mortified."

He took his hand off the gear shift and patted my hand. "Don't be. She'd love to meet you."

My eyes darted to his. "Uh, okay."

He grinned. "You know. When it's time."

"Right."

Lex cut off three cars to pull off the M1 and slid onto the surface streets of central London. His driving became even more haphazard, and I closed my eyes so I didn't have to watch.

"Abbie, do you feel sick?"

I shook my head. "No. Your driving just scares me a little."

Alexi chuckled. "Remind me not to take you to Italy or Germany then. I drive slow here in comparison."

My heart leapt at the idea of traveling together, but my brain tamped it down. Just because he no longer had a fiancée didn't mean we'd be riding off into the sunset together. We still had a few things to work out.

Suddenly, Lex swerved into an alley and stopped the car.

I looked around. "Are we hiding from paparazzi?"

He laughed as he shook his head. "No. This is the VIP entrance. I'd still like to keep tonight about us and not the side show, if I can."

Out of nowhere, a tall Asian man in a dark suit appeared and opened my door for me. I stepped out, and my breath caught as I stood next to him. He was huge. Not just tall, but also massively wide.

When he spoke, his voice was all polished Brit. "Good evening, Miss Nartey, Mr. Chase. I trust you'll have a pleasant evening."

Lex led me through the side door, and immediately the aroma of delicious food assailed me. Ginger and garlic were the first scents to make my mouth water. "Wow. I want whatever smells that good."

"You'll have to be more specific," Lex said with a smile. "It all does."

The hostess appeared in the candlelit hallway and led us to a private table. There were no other patrons in the room, but when I leaned back, I could see into the main restaurant, and the place was packed. I also had a view to the street, and there was a small hoard of people waiting outside. "Where are we, exactly?"

"It's this new Vietnamese fusion place called Pho. I know the owner, so I called in a favor."

Once seated, I leaned forward. "I know it's uncouth or whatever to ask this, but sometimes you just gotta know. Just how do you *know* all these people? And how many favors do they owe you?"

He laughed. "Andrew, my mate from University, is the owner. He spent a summer trekking through Vietnam and fell in love with the culture and the people. Eventually he married a Vietnamese woman. They moved back here and opened the restaurant."

"Wow. It's a beautiful place. Is he your age?"

"No, he's a little older. We used to play cricket together."

Cricket. Right. I shifted uncomfortably at the thought of just how little I knew about him.

Waiters brought around tea, and Alexi ordered our drinks for us. Once drinks had arrived and our food orders were put in, he sat back and studied me, a slight crease forming in his forehead. "You have to tell me. Is this too much, not enough? I'm finding you very hard to read right now."

I was hard to read? "Oh, no, it's fantastic. Faith and Sophie mentioned this place when they took me to Camberwell to hide me last weekend. We were looking to do a girls' night, but they said it was impossible to get in this place. So it's really nice to be able to actually eat here. I'll have to remember all the flavors so I can tell them. Sophie, of course, will insist that we try to recreate the meals. For someone who doesn't cook, she's really adventurous in the kitchen."

He frowned slightly. "Your friends aren't exactly fans of mine, are they?"

I hadn't prepared for that question. "No, it's not that. I think they were unhappy that I lied to them about who I was seeing, and they worry about me. Especially Sophie. But Faith is in your corner. Sophie will come around."

He winced. "Abbie, about—"

The first course of hot soup arrived, and my stomach grumbled as the aromas of ginger and onions hit my nostrils. "Wow, I didn't realize I was so hungry. Faith kept trying to feed me before I left since we weren't sure where you were taking me for dinner."

He laughed, and it softened the edginess in his gaze. "She thought I'd be starving you?"

"No. More like she thought we'd be going somewhere pretty but where the food wasn't very good, or the portion sizes would only be enough to feed a size-zero anorexic model."

He laughed. "Oh, no. I pay attention. I even made sure

nothing has mushrooms in it. And I've seen you eat, remember?"

I flushed at the memory of the weekend we spent together and the way I'd devoured the breakfast he made me. "Yeah, I'd forgotten about that."

"I remembered."

I met his gaze. Time to bite the bullet. If I didn't do it now, I'd get caught up in the romance, and I still had questions I needed answered. "So last Sunday, you said you couldn't tell me anything about what was going on with you for another week. Can you tell me now?"

He wiped his mouth with his napkin then gently placed it back in his lap. I couldn't help but marvel at his impeccable table manners. Of course, he'd probably had a lifetime to learn all of the appropriate spoons and forks. All I'd really learned was to start on the outside and work my way inward.

He cleared his throat. "It all had to do with work, really."

My brows shot up. "So, what is it you do, anyway? I don't think you've actually told me."

His smile was bright and warmed me. "Well, as of Monday, I will no longer be the owner of the Take Back the Night software application."

"What happens on Monday? Are you leaving?"

His mouth tightened, but then he answered smoothly, "No. Final sale of my company goes through. Then I'll just be the acting CEO until they can get someone else to fill my shoes."

My mouth fell open. "Wow. I had no idea."

"How could you? I didn't exactly tell you." He took a sip of his scotch. "You weren't supposed to have an idea. If anybody had a clue and leaked it, the deal would have been off. Hell, it's still supposed to be a secret until Monday."

"Why?"

"My father, for one. If he finds out about the deal, he'll try for a hostile snatch of my company."

I blinked, and my hand fluttered to my chest. "Wow. Is your relationship that contentious?"

"Yeah, you could say that. It's always been like that. He prefers Xander. Xander fights less. Dad tells him to do something, and he nods and smiles then does what he likes. I fight more." Lex shrugged.

He went silent as the waiters reappeared and removed our soup bowls. Once they filled the table with heaping piles of dumplings, rice, and succulent smelling stews, they vanished and left the two of us alone again.

Only then did Alexi continue. "Mum is the one with the titles and the inherited wealth. Dad only got his wealth from leveraging Mum's connections, her name, and Grandad's money. It works for him, and he pretends to love me. I stopped trying to figure out my parents or why my father sees me as the bane of his existence."

"That must be hard."

He shrugged. "No harder than having parents who don't support you. At least I have my mum."

"But you didn't tell her about the job?"

He gave a sharp shake of his head. "No. She wouldn't have meant to let anything slip, but it's easy to not be paying attention and out comes something pivotal."

"Must be lonely keeping so much to yourself. Do you have anyone to confide in?"

"Nick, Gem. Sometimes Xander." He gazed at me through lowered lashes. "Now you."

I flushed. "I'm sure you have other people you can confide in besides me. There were three hundred people at your birthday party, for the love of God."

Alexi shook his head, dislodging a dark lock that fell over his brow. "There are a lot of people who want the fun and the lifestyle and stand around wanting to be part of the entourage. I'd rather be on my own at my house, honestly. It sucks. I never know who I can trust or who just wants to be my friend because of who my cousins are or because of what they think I can do for them."

My heart broke for the loneliness he must have felt. "No wonder you didn't tell me who you are."

He winced. "I didn't think you were like that. Pretty much after talking to you the first time, I knew you weren't. I've just never had anybody close to me."

Tears pricked my eyelids, and I blinked them away rapidly. "Thank you for telling me," I murmured. "What happens now? After the sale of the company? And what does the company do, anyway?"

His eyes gleamed. "Well, Nick and I built software that connects all the elite clubs, restaurants, bars, and lounges in one place. Kind of a social calendar for the fabulous set. Then we expanded it to include certain VIP accesses that aren't accessible to everyone. We worked out a deal with all the Club Membership places like China White to allow temporary memberships for anyone we send them, for a cut, of course. And we keep it super exclusive. Anyone who wants access has to pay a pretty penny, and there's only a set number of all-access passes. So for any given weekend, there will be two passes per club, or restaurant, or lounge, or show, or something. It's first come, first served. Tonight, at midnight, for example, we'll release all the availability for next week's venues. Sometimes we crash the system with all the people trying to get on. We eventually expanded to concerts, and then included lower access things like events and restaurants." The excitement was clear in his expression, the way he gesticulated with his hands. He loved what he did and was really proud.

Wow. In a million years I never would have thought of that. "That's huge. I know lots of people who'd kill to get into the places you have access to. Hell, I'm a bit awed by it all. I wouldn't want to do it on a constant basis, but they sure are fun once in a while."

"Yeah, going out in London has proved to be a lucrative business." He smiled ruefully. "Not bad for the kid who was never going to amount to much."

"Maybe your father will surprise you. He should be proud."

"Well, he won't be."

"I'm sorry," I said softly.

"For what?"

How could I explain that, even before I'd known about who he really was, I'd judged him? "For not seeing past the shine. I'm probably no better than the people you were talking about."

He took my hand. "Well, you weren't working on all the information, and you knew something was off." He squeezed my hand. "I should have told you from the start."

"I guess I understand why you didn't."

"I know it's a lot to ask, but I'd like another chance. I feel terrible for how things turned out for you. I wish I'd just told you so you could have prepared or something."

"It's okay. It's not like I would have done anything differently. I knew you were different the minute I laid eyes on you." I raked my teeth over my bottom lip.

A smile tugged at his lips. "Then let me help you out with school. It's my fault your parents freaked out on you."

I shook my head and took my hand back. "Alexi, no. I was serious when I said I need to figure it out on my own." And that was true. But why did I suddenly feel nauseous thinking about it.

His brow furrowed. "You have to accept help sometimes."

I took a sip of water to cool my dry, itchy throat. "And I am. I actually have gotten a few photography gigs. A couple of the models that rent from Max have had me taking pictures for them. Jasper too. If I can keep it up, I can pay for school and my living expenses all by myself."

His lips flattened. "You really won't let me help?"

"Nope." I shook my head.

He shook his head. "I really wish you would."

I inhaled deeply, praying for the lightheaded and hot feeling to dissipate. I refused to be sick on this date. *Refused.* "I know. And it's sweet that you want to, but no. Mom and Dad pulling the plug was maybe the thing I needed. If they hadn't yanked my world out from under me, I would forever be beholden. Right now, I'm sort of free. I don't have to take any bullshit. I'm not obligated to listen, and there won't be any guilt when I don't." I paused. "Or at least not much." The skin on my arms prickled with a flash of heat and I swallowed hard.

He nodded. "I understand the need to be free." Lex took a sip of his drink and slid his hand across the table to take mine. "Abbie. There's something I wanted to talk to you about."

Lex's eyes were so serious, and his voice was grave. I tried to focus on his voice, but the scratchy feeling at the back of my throat distracted me. "What is it?"

"I don't know how to say this, so I'll just—" He paused. Studying me, he frowned. "Abbie, are you okay?"

"Uhm, fine. It's just a little hot in here. My throat's a bit scratchy, but it's nothing. What do you want to say?"

He narrowed his gaze and studied me closely. "Hell. I'm so sorry."

"What are you talking about?"

"I think you're having an allergic reaction."

"Don't be crazy. I'm fine. It's just a little hot in here."

His brows shot up. "Really, then why are your lips swelling?"

CHAPTER SEVENTEEN

ABBIE

Two hours after the dinner debacle, Alexi held me close and watched me sleep. After using my EpiPen, I'd refused to go home. I'd also been livid that he insisted on paramedics coming to check me out.

But they'd told him the same thing I had. All I needed was rest. So, he took me home. To his bed. I was half asleep when we'd come in, so he hadn't even had a chance to show me his place properly since all the repairs had been done. I changed into a T-shirt and climbed into his arms as if I'd been doing so for years.

Alexi held me tighter even as he cursed himself for being all kinds of an idiot. He'd called ahead and made sure none of the food had mushrooms in it, but he'd completely forgotten about the condiments and sauces. "Stupid, stupid," he muttered softly.

I stirred in his arms. "You're holding on pretty tight there."

He only loosened his grip marginally. "Sorry. I was really worried about you."

I turned in his arms. "And I told you that you didn't need to be." I gestured to my face. "See, I'm already back to normal. I'm fine. It happens."

"But it happened on my watch. And I told you I'd called ahead, so you were less careful about what you were eating. I feel like an arse. I was trying to impress you."

"Hey," I reached up to cup his face, "All I wanted was you tonight. I didn't need impressing."

I kissed him gently. Despite everything, his body went on instant alert. Ready to rock as if he'd been plugged into an electrical socket. "Abbie, you should be getting some rest."

I met his gaze with a direct one of my own. "I'd rather make love to you, if you don't mind. I've missed you."

He dragged in a ragged breath. With shaking hands, he caressed my cheek. "I've been dreaming of having you here in my house, in my bed, since I rescued you from that Mini Cooper."

I ducked my head. "Of course you would remember that. So embarrassing. Must happen to every single green Yank who shows up on your shores."

Alexi put his finger under my chin and tilted my head, forcing me to look at him. "Don't be embarrassed. I fell for that girl who wanted to save her camera and yanked me down with her to save its life."

"Well, that camera is my everything. A girl's gotta eat." Quietly, I added, "When you pulled me into your lap, I thought you Brit boys took chivalry to a whole new level."

Alexi gently drew me to his body.

I drew in a shuddering breath as I came into contact with his erection. "Alexi, I—"

He pulled back and kissed my temple, then whispered, "Shh, it's okay. We don't have to do anything."

I shook my head. "I was going to say that I feel safe with you."

Wait, I trusted him? After everything he'd put me through? Again, he kissed me, his tongue sliding over mine, exploring my mouth. I sucked on his tongue, and he shivered. I laced my hands through his hair and lightly scored my nails into his scalp. A shudder racked his body. His erection throbbed against my belly, and I smiled against his lips.

"Jesus, Abbie."

I sat up in bed. With one hand, I reached between us and started unbuttoning his shirt. One by one, the tiny silver buttons slipped from their loops, revealing tanned skin and muscles beneath. I'd seen him without his shirt on often enough to know just how hard those muscles were and where tattoos lay hidden. I loved the Sanskrit etching on his ribs, but my favorite was the expansive eagle wings on his back. I loved how his muscles would ripple when I ran my fingertips over them.

Drawing back from our kiss, I tucked both hands into his shirt and pushed it off his shoulders. It fell to the ground without making a sound.

He reached for me and tugged his T-shirt off of me, leaving me bare.

I went for his trousers next, my trembling hands working on the buckle of his belt. All the while, his gaze burned on me intensely, scorching my exposed flesh.

His hands lightly caressed my face then traced a path down to my breasts. The backs of his fingertips just barely grazed my flesh. When they reached my nipples, he let the pad of his thumbs trace over the puckered tips. When he circled the sensitive tips again, a moan tore from my throat as a stab of pleasure hit me deep in my center.

"You're so responsive, Abbie. Just one touch, and you're melting already."

His pants followed his discarded shirt, and he wiggled out of them. All that stood between us were his boxer briefs and the slip of my barely there satin panties. I curled into his embrace once more and kissed his chest. His muscles bunched, and his chest vibrated with a low rumble when I flicked my tongue over his nipple.

"A-Abbie..." His breath was ragged and raw.

Tentatively, as I kissed my way across his chest, I slid a hand down his body, over each rippled ab, down to his straining erection. Lightly, my fingertips explored the rigid length through his shorts. His hands froze in my hair, but he didn't stop me.

More emboldened, I slipped my hand into the waistband of his shorts then wrapped my fingers around his girth and lightly tested the weight of him. With the contact of flesh on flesh, he shuddered then hissed, and his grip on my braids tightened. I stroked him, slowly running my thumb over the tip of his erection, and his hips bucked. I smiled up at him and stroked him again.

His jaw clenched, and a vivid curse tore out through gnashed teeth. I immediately stilled, and a whimper escaped his lips.

"God, Abbie. You feel so goooood." His voice was hoarse, raw.

I wrapped my hand around him once more, and he hissed again. This time I brought my free hand to his chest and explored the smooth skin of his nipple with my thumb, just as he'd done to me.

His eyes drifted closed, and he moaned deep and low as I explored. His nipple puckered just like mine did when he touched me. Alexi dropped his forehead to mine and whispered, "You feel so good. But I need you to stop."

I stilled immediately. "I thought you liked—"

He chuckled harshly. "God, yes. I like it. I'm just trying to slow us down before I lose total control here."

"I think I'd like to see that." I pumped again twice and smiled as his whole body shook. But when his gaze met mine, I knew he'd lost the battle for control.

❦

Lex

Gently, I slid my tongue over her lower lip, and she parted her lips for me. For several minutes the only sound that pierced the silence in the room was our moans and muffled whispers.

I shifted our position so that she lay propped against the pillows on the bed. "I've been missing you."

A shy smile stole across her lips. "I missed you too."

"I never meant to hurt you."

She nodded. "I know."

When I kissed her again, my tongue was possessive,

staking a claim on her as my hands moved over her naked flesh. My thumbs traced each of her ribs before my hands travelled up and I traced over her nipples.

Abbie writhed beneath me, and with each wiggle of her hips, the blood rushed louder in my head. And the whispers grew to a thunder. *Take her. She's yours. Don't let go.*

She blinked up at me, eyes wide. "Alexi, I know what I want. And it's you. It's always been you."

I rolled off of her for a split second and snagged a condom from my bedside table. In less than a minute, I had it on and pulled her to me, kissing her softly. "Abbie, you are incredible."

As I slid into her warm depths, the words *I love you* lingered on the edge of my consciousness like an ethereal dream I couldn't catch. I rocked into her over and over again, and she scored her nails on my back, calling my name on breathy little sighs. Even if I couldn't grab hold of the words, I knew I couldn't ever walk away from her.

I knew the moment she skyrocketed into orgasm because her body clamped onto me like a vice. Unable to withstand the pleasure that chased up my spine, I followed her into oblivion.

Holding her tightly to me afterward, I kissed her temple. "I've wanted you here from the moment you danced with me that first night."

Abbie giggled. "God, I was so nervous."

"Why?"

"Have you seen you? And you could dance." She lifted the sheet to look down my body. "I mean, what's a girl to do?"

"I can think of a few things." I laughed.

"You're incorrigible."

"Who me?" I kissed her softly, ignoring the prick of guilt. She was so happy, so relaxed. What would happen when I told her?

Casually dropped it into conversation about Silas, what he'd done to us. What I'd had to do to protect my brother.

As if that was going to work out in my favor.

You have to tell her.

Soon. I'd tell her soon. But not quite yet. I needed to live in this blissful existence for just a little bit longer.

You're a liar.

I shoved aside the internal thoughts and prickling guilt. "So, what are you doing Sunday?"

She winced. "Ugh, I'm headed to campus. Xander's helping me with some of my portrait work. I have a few things I want to show him before class on Monday. And I'd rather get his opinion before I print them all out. Why? What's happening?"

"I want to take you to meet my mother."

She sat up, dislodging the sheet covering her breasts. "What? Your mother?"

I did try to focus on her face, but her breasts were *right there*. I licked one nipple, and Abbie immediately melted, laying back on the bed.

"Yes, my mother. I want to show you off," I whispered.

"Okay. I'll come. But I have nothing to wear."

"You can go like this, for all I care. As long as you're by my side."

"As if." She chewed her lip. "What if she doesn't like me? Approve or whatever."

"She'll l—" I clamped my mouth shut. I'd nearly said my mother would love her almost as much as I did. I did love her, but before I told her that, I needed to tell her the truth. I'd wanted to do it tonight. But then she'd gotten sick. And now, I wanted to hold onto her for one more night before I might lose her for good. "She'll think you're perfect."

CHAPTER EIGHTEEN

ABBIE

I leaned into Alexi as he kissed me hard and long at my back door. He lingered over my lips and sighed. For once, the gray that blanketed London the majority of the time had parted to reveal some sunshine, and it backlit his beautiful face.

"I need to go before one of your neighbors sees me and calls the paparazzi."

I moaned. "You could come inside." Through the sweats I wore and his jeans, I could feel the ridge of his arousal.

He dropped his forehead to mine. "Woman, you are insatiable. You'd think after last night, and this morning, and then the shower, I'd have tired you out by now."

I grinned. I was exhausted, but it didn't stop me from wanting him again. "What can I say? I can't get enough."

"Jesus, Abbie." He kissed my nose. "I want to. Which is why I probably shouldn't. You have work to do and a roommate to deconstruct with, and I have some work to do with Nick. But I will see you tomorrow, okay?"

I sighed. "Right. We can't just avoid our lives entirely. I need to start putting out my resume too. The photography gigs are good. But I think I also need another job."

His jaw tightened. "I'm trying really hard to respect your wishes, but it's getting harder. I'm the reason you're in this mess."

I kissed him softly. "It's not a mess. It's me getting to live my life how I see fit. So, no. No rushing in and doing the prince charming bit. No pun intended."

He grinned and kissed me once more before heading to his car.

Still a little lust drunk, I tripped up the stairs and let myself in to my flat. Faith looked up expectantly with a wide smile on her face. Sophie was also home for once, but she didn't seem nearly as enthused.

I slid my shoes off in the hall before skipping into the living room.

"Someone's in a good mood," Sophie said quietly.

I couldn't help grinning again.

"Wouldn't you be in a good mood if you'd spent the night having one of London's most eligible bachelors catering to your every sexual whim?" Faith gave me a pointed look. "You, go shower, change, then come out and tell us all the sordid details. I want to know skill level, size, and dexterity, all of it. Don't you dare leave anything out."

I giggled. "But I'm so tired. Can't I just sit here and rest for a minute?" I'd had a shower at Alexi's this morning, but I could use the change of clothes. Though his sweats were so worn in and soft, they felt like heaven.

"Yes, yes you may. And have a crumpet while you tease

us with all your delicious sex-having."

Sophie passed over the tray of crumpets, and I took one gratefully. When I took a bite, the sinful delight of warm jam melting on my tongue made me moan. I hadn't realized just how hungry I was. I'd had some fruit at Alexi's, but I'd been so nervous and keyed up and on a lust high that I hadn't eaten much.

I glanced at Faith. "So, where do you want me to start?"

Faith rolled her eyes. "Start from the minute you left this flat."

As I gave them a rundown of the night, Faith sat forward in her seat while Sophie sat back picking at her nail polish. I understood Sophie was concerned for me, but she didn't need to ruin my fun. "So yeah, then he brought me home just now."

"When are you seeing him again?" Faith asked

"Well, he's got some work to do today. He also wants to be around for Jasper's photo shoot. He wasn't too enthused to hear we'd slept together."

Finally, Sophie leaned forward. "Does he believe there's something between you and Jasper? *Is* there something between you and Jasper?"

I shook my head and rolled my eyes. "No. Not really, and no, not at all. In that order. Jasper's just been a great friend."

Sophie frowned then slouched back again. "If you say so."

I ignored her. "And Alexi wants me to meet his mother tomorrow."

Faith's jaw dropped. "Are you serious? That's huge. This is insane."

Sophie frowned. "What are you going to wear?"

"No idea. But I can't think about that right now. It'll just make me too nervous." I changed the subject. "So, Faith, you promised me spillage of your innermost when I got back. I'm back now. You want to tell us what happened with Liam?"

Faith groaned and covered her face with the pillow. "I'd rather talk about you and Sexy Lexi and lovely things. I don't want to talk about how awful Dublin was."

I handed her a crumpet from the tray. "Here, eat for fortification. Then spill."

Faith took a tentative bite before she finally said. "Dublin was awful. Horrible actually."

"Honey, why didn't you say anything?" I asked.

"What happened?" Asked Sophie, back in friend mode.

Faith shrugged. "It's not something I can put my finger on really. It wasn't that different from any other trip I've had up there." She tucked her blond hair behind her ear. "Okay, look, when he's down here, Liam is charming, freer. Fun. We go out, we talk. But when I went up there to see him, it was stilted. Awkward. He won't even hold my hand in public. It's pretty hard to talk about how we end the long-distance thing when I can barely get him to say two words to me."

Sophie frowned. "That's bizarre. You guys are always so touchy feely. Most of the time it's really embarrassing for other people."

"I know, right?" Faith exclaimed.

"What do you think it could be?" I asked as I tucked my feet underneath me. "Do you think he didn't want you there?"

"Well, I think he's got some secret girlfriend or something

up there, and I told him such."

Sophie snorted. "Oh, Faith, you did not?"

"Oh, yes I did. I went full-on crazy girlfriend on him and accused him of having a whole other life."

I chewed my lip. "And how did that go?"

"He laughed me off and made me think I was losing my mind."

I patted her knee. "Oh, honey, I'm sure it's not like that."

"Well, it's like something. The rest of the weekend was filled with this awkward silence."

"I'm sorry," I muttered.

"Yeah, anyway, so I came back, and then everything pretty much went tits up with you and Lex, and honestly I didn't want to talk about it. I was hoping it would all blow over when Liam came here, but then I got to thinking that I didn't want a boyfriend who treated me like I was a crazy person. I wanted a boyfriend who wanted to fix the root of the problem."

I frowned. "So, what happened in that bathroom, Faith?"

"Honestly, I don't know what happened with Angel. I mean, there I was, staring at his bare ass, and I couldn't take my eyes off of him."

I shook my head. "I didn't even know you were that into him."

Faith shook her head. "I think it was less about him than it was about me needing something else. I haven't been that happy with Liam for a while. Then when Angel turned around and asked if I saw something I liked, I could barely move."

I blinked rapidly. Had I been presented with a specimen

as fine as Angel, I might not have refused either. "So, what? You just jumped him in the shower? That is so not like you."

Sophie laughed for the first time since I had come home. "No, that sounds like me."

"Maybe I was channeling you, I guess." Faith giggled. "But I didn't have sex with him. We just snogged. There was *a lot* of snogging."

I collapsed in a fit of giggles. "So, you're making out fully clothed with him fully naked. I'm sorry, but I have to ask, how did you not get distracted by his... uhm..." My voice trailed.

Faith barked out a laugh. "Well, it wasn't easy. I mean, it was right there, and rather insistent, and did I mention big?"

Sophie leaned forward. "Just how big are we talking?" She put up her hands with space between them. When Faith shook her head, Sophie adjusted her hands. Faith giggled, then moved her hands even further apart. Sophie's eyes bulged. "I'm going to have to try to convince Max that we need an open relationship or something. I can't believe there's a beautiful boy with equipment that large, and I can't sample the goods."

Faith and I howled with laughter. Faith clutched her side and said. "The thing is, he's lovely too. At one point he stopped and said, 'So, are we taking off your clothes, or are we just going to continue this later?'"

"He can be so sweet. I told you guys how he took care of me on that shoot, made sure the models listened, and then introduced me around until I had a couple of other jobs lined up. He's lovely. You could do worse."

"I don't know. I don't think I'm really looking for another

relationship."

Sophie groaned before plopping back against the pillows. "You mean you're not even going to fully sample the goods?"

"Not sure yet. He wants to hang out or something, so we're going to go to Jasper's show on Friday. I'll see after that. I'm trying to keep to casual."

"At least tell me the kissing was good," Sophie mumbled.

Faith narrowed her eyes. "I was making out with him fully clothed while he was in the shower. What do you think?"

I couldn't help but laugh. How had I missed this? I'd been so caught up in my personal melodrama that I hadn't had enough girl time. I needed to change that. I didn't want to spend all my time in London with a boy. No matter how sexy he was. "So, then you told Liam?"

Mid-bite of my crumpet, I heard the Skype ringing on my computer. Excusing myself, I ran into the room and swore I would skip the masochistic torture if it was my parents or Easton. I smiled when I saw it was Ama.

I hit the video button and grinned when I saw my sister's broad smile. "Hey, Ama."

Ama sighed with relief. "I have to tell you, I wasn't sure if you'd answer for me. No one's been able to get a hold of you, so I thought I was *persona non grata* too."

Of all my family, Ama was the only one who had ever supported any of my decisions. Which was why she was my favorite sister. "Of course not. I always answer your calls."

"Glad to hear it. Now, give it to me straight. How are you?"

I shrugged. "Actually, not bad. Could be better, of course,

but I'm working my ass off and finally getting somewhere in my class. I was convinced my professor hated me, but now I think he's beginning to respect my work."

"And friends, you've got a good support system over there? I worried about you when that whole tabloid thing went down."

I frowned. Yeah, that whole tabloid thing and the subsequent abandonment by my parents. "I'm okay. I've got some pretty good friends. Faith and Sophie were pretty stellar. They whisked me off to Sophie's boyfriend's house for a few days to hide out from the paparazzi, and they kept me fed with proper food and only the occasional tub of ice cream. Oh yeah, and loads of scones and clotted cream."

"Well, you look fantastic. Or does that fabulous glow have more to do with that guy than your fabulous friends?"

I ducked my head. "Maybe a little bit of both. But mostly it's this city. The whole place is alive, Ama. I mean it just screams with energy. I can't help but feel creative here. It's pretty awesome. It's like I'm where I'm supposed to be. Like this is my home, and it has nothing to do with family, or friends, or school, but more to do with..." I paused, my voice trailing. "...with how it makes me feel every morning when I wake up, regardless of what else is going on. There's just something about this city."

Ama smiled. "You look really happy, little sister."

"I am happy." I shrugged. "That's not to say it's easy, because it's not. Alexi drives me up the wall, and Xander is really demanding, and Faith and Sophie have their own problems that I have to be a better friend for, and I'm struggling with the job thing, but it's still pretty unbelievable."

"Speaking of the job thing, I'm working on Mom and Dad, okay? You just keep doing what you're doing. I'll find a way to have them support you, or at least pay for the rest of school. It's not right or fair what they've done."

Tears stung my eyes. "Ama, I appreciate you trying for me, but it won't change them. And come to think of it, I don't want the strings that come with that money. I *want* to do this on my own. It was a mistake to count on them in the first place."

"Stop it." My sister's voice took on a hard edge. "You earned every penny of that money. You got the same deal the rest of us got when you were ten. As long as you worked hard and kept your grades above a B average, you would never have to worry about school expenses. They reneged just because they didn't like your new boyfriend, or whatever. It's wrong."

"It's also their prerogative."

"Abbie."

"No, Ama, even if they brought me a briefcase full of money in small, unmarked bills and not a single string attached, I wouldn't take it."

"Abbie, don't be stubborn."

I rolled my shoulders, unsure how to make her see what I was talking about. "Look, you were the only one who believed I could do this. You've supported me from the beginning. And I appreciate that. But *I* need to know I can do this and do it on my own. I don't want to look back years from now and cringe, wondering if I could have done it, was it possible? Those invisible strings would tug at my psyche for years. I don't want that. I want to be able to stand on my own without them. I'm all about being surrounded by the positive right now. And their money stinks of, 'You can't possibly be successful at this. Come home so you can be monitored properly.' If I don't stand up to them now, it's never going to happen."

Amar's shoulders slumped. "Okay, I understand, but at least let me help you. I've got some money tucked away for a rainy day."

"Are you kidding, Ama? You're a second-year resident. Keep your money."

"Abbie!"

I shook my head. "No, Ama, not even from you. I was serious about doing this on my own. Lex even offered, and I turned him down."

"You're being stubborn, Abbie."

I grinned at her. "I hear it's a family trait."

"Okay, fine, but the moment you need anything, you call me. Don't you dare call them first. Do you hear me? I'll do whatever I can to help you. You look so much happier now than you ever did at home. Like you're a more vibrant version of yourself. I don't ever want to see that go away, so I'll do anything you need."

I sniffed and blinked rapidly, trying to stave off the threatening emotional downpour.

"Thank you, Ama. I don't know what I would do without you."

She grinned. "I imagine you'd be just fine. Now, when are you going to tell me about this boyfriend of yours? And can he kiss? Because those pictures suggest that he sure as hell can."

CHAPTER NINETEEN

ABBIE

I licked my lips nervously as I walked into Xander's office. As usual, his desk and shelves were cluttered with cameras and photography books. His desk had images and magazines stacked high, and I could forget about sitting—there wasn't a clean surface anywhere. I grabbed a stack of photos off the chair and placed them on the already cluttered desk. I handed him my memory card. "I appreciate you taking the time to review these with me before class."

"Of course. I want you to succeed, and I'm glad you've taken my advice and done some work on some portraits."

Quietly, he studied my images frame by frame, taking his time. I wasn't looking forward to another verbal flaying from him. But I'd worked hard on these and needed his feedback.

I'd taken a whole series of photographs of London's street performers. The dancers and the musicians and the singers. Most of the locations had been simple enough. All I had to do was sit on the tube long enough, and I'd catch someone playing or singing. I always tipped heavily, unlike many of the Londoners.

With a few, I'd also been lucky enough to catch the movement of the trains behind us or the hustle and bustle of moving commuters blurring out the landscape. These shots were good. They were better than good. My favorite was of an old man playing the violin as uniformed school children raced around him at the park. I'd caught the sea of burgundy uniforms in the background of the photo.

When he was done, Xander sat back and studied me. His first words weren't about my photos though. "I wanted to see how you were doing."

I frowned. "I'm fine."

"Well, I know about the shit with the paparazzi. Is it getting in the way of doing your work?"

I sighed. So this was about Alexi. "No. I'm fine. And as you can see, my work hasn't suffered. Save that one assignment." I stiffened my back. "Is this the part where you tell me I should probably stay away from your brother? Or did you have something school related to discuss?" I clamped my jaw tight as I seethed.

He sighed and pinched the bridge of his nose. "Okay, look. I was out of line to tell you to stay away from Lex. I, uhm, was surprised that you knew him. And I sort of overreacted. I won't lie and say that you don't intrigue me. Probably more than you should."

"I thought you had a very firm policy against sleeping with your students."

He chuckled and leaned forward. "Yes, well. In case you

haven't guessed, I'm pretty good at bending the rules to suit myself."

I folded my arms. "Honestly, I'm not sure why I fascinate you so much. I'm just a girl. A prickly one at that. You're Xander Chase. I'm sure you don't want for women."

"I am Xander Chase. And you're right; a woman in my bed isn't something that's particularly hard to come by. But finding one with a brain and a heart and inner strength with attitude to spare, well, it's a bit difficult."

I shifted uncomfortably in my seat and wished I had my camera in my hands. I'd never had to turn down so much male attention before. I met his gaze. "Alexi."

He nodded. "Yes, Alexi." Xander's smile was faint and a little sad. "He's my brother, and I suspect you love him."

I squared my shoulders. "I'm not a toy you can fight over. Besides, you're my professor. I came here to learn from you. You can make or break my career, and I need you."

His jaw ticked. "You make him happy, so I'll be the teacher you need. Your work today was exceptional. I expect it to continue improving. No more hiccups?"

I shoved the swell of pride into a box to examine later. "No more hiccups. I'm here to work." Then, I added, "I also expect to be treated like any other one of your students. No more random acts of flirtation and no more singling me out. The others are beginning to notice."

His eyes narrowed imperceptibly, and he crossed his arms, leaning back in his chair. "Random acts of flirtation?"

Oh no. He would not do that guy thing where he made me feel like I was being crazy. I'd sensed something there. "Yeah, like at the club and at the pub the other night."

He nodded slowly. "Fair enough. I can manage that."

"Thank you."

Xander indicated his computer. "Your photos. They're excellent. Some of them are really exquisite. I think you have a real knack for portraits."

I had to keep from grinning like an idiot as the warmth of his praise swept through me. "Really? You're not just saying that?"

"Really. I don't blow smoke up anyone's arse, no matter how nicely they ask. Now go on. I suspect you have something far more interesting to do with your Sunday than sit in this cramped office. I'll see you in class on Monday."

As I stood and walked out, I could feel him watching me.

ABBIE

Later that afternoon, I attempted to tug my hand out of Alexi's. "I'm not sure about this. This is your time with your family. I feel like I'm intruding."

He squeezed my hand. "Would you relax? You were *invited*."

I chewed my lip. "She didn't invite me specifically. She just said she'd like to meet me sometime."

Lex paused and turned to face me as we stood on the steps of his mother's Kensington townhome. "She'll love you. And would you stop all that nonsense? You *are* my girlfriend."

His girlfriend. I loved the sound of that. But there was a tightness around his mouth. Something in his bright smile was a little off. Like he *needed* this visit to go well. I still couldn't let it go. "Maybe we should take some time. You know, let me meet your mother on a different day. Another time."

He only laughed. "You're my girlfriend. I want to tell everybody I know. I want to show you off. And it's important to me that you meet my family. Can you do this for me?"

I shifted from foot to foot and tucked one of my braids behind my ears. "I'm just not very good at this stuff. Parental units make me squigy."

He shook his head. "I'm not even sure that's a word. I doubt that would hold up in Scrabble."

"Oh, but I think it would. Like Beyoncé, I'm adding words to the dictionary. You'll see. Before long, it'll be in Webster's."

His response—kissing me soundly on the mouth. He lingered before pulling back. He started to speak then paused, looking as if he might say something. He seemed to rethink before finally saying, "She'll love you. I know it."

I nodded, wanting to trust him. Besides, after my own parents, how bad could Stephanie Chase be?

Lex let us into the spacious townhome without ringing the doorbell first. I tried not to stare or touch anything as I stepped into the marble foyer. Bright paintings hung on the walls, adding bold splashes of color to the otherwise stark white of the interior. Two curving staircases framed the entrance, leading to a landing nearly obscured by the lavish chandelier. I craned my head up and gasped. The ceiling had been painted with a heaven-scape of pink and orange clouds.

"Wow, it's beautiful."

"I'm glad you like it." At the banister at the top of the stairs stood Stephanie Chase.

I gaped at her. Her dark hair hung to her waist in beautiful waves, and she wore minimal makeup. She'd dressed much as I had, with skinny jeans and a body-hugging sweater. Though, instead of boots, her feet were bare.

Lex squeezed my hand. "Mum, I have someone I'd like you to meet."

Stephanie glided down the stairs with a beaming smile for her son. I tried not to feel bereft at the loss of his warm, reassuring hand when he let go to hug his mother. Instead, I slapped what I hoped was an intelligent, put-together-girlfriend smile on my face.

Stephanie hugged Alexi tight before stepping back to scrutinize him. "You look happy, Lex."

"Well, that has a lot to do with Abbie." He reached out his hand for me, and I automatically took it. "Abena Nartey, this is my mother, Stephanie Chase. Mum, this is Abbie."

"Why don't you come in and have a seat?"

After Stephanie had dispatched the maid for tea, I fidgeted on the snow-white couch with Lex. *I can do this, I can do this, I can do this.* How hard could it be? All I had to do was sit there and smile and answer some questions. I cleared my throat. "Your home is beautiful, Mrs. Chase." I frowned. "Or, erm, Your Majesty."

Stephanie waved her hand dismissively as she smiled warmly. "No, dear, I insist you call me Stephanie."

I gave her a tight smile. I wouldn't be calling her anything then. After all, my strict cultural upbringing dictated the only appropriate address as Mrs. or Auntie for an elder, particularly my boyfriend's mother. But I'd deal with that later. Right now, I had to get through this.

"So, my son tells me you're a photographer."

I nodded slowly, and Alexi squeezed my hand in encouragement. I forced myself to breathe. "I'm studying now under your son Xander."

Stephanie laughed. "Oh, Xander, that naughty little upstart. He doesn't visit as often as he should. I do hope he hasn't been giving you a hard time. He's a bit notorious."

"I will tell him when I see him next class." I liked Stephanie Chase and could see where Alexi got his heart from. "You must be very proud. His work is extraordinary and inspiring."

The older woman beamed. "I *am* proud of him. I'm proud of both my boys. They've been through so much and have turned out so well."

I could feel my smile falter. Alexi had only told me about his contentious relationship with his father. Was there more he'd left out? *Calm down, you two have no more secrets. When you're alone, just ask him what she means.*

I coughed. "I, uhm, I—"

"You don't have to search for the tactful response, darling. I know Alexander can be a handful."

I cleared my throat. "Yes, I noticed. But he really is an excellent teacher."

Alexi squeezed my hand. "Stop putting her on the spot, Mum."

Stephanie laughed. "I'm sorry, darling, I'll behave."

I squeezed his hand. "It's okay. I'm fine, I promise."

"So, what do you two love birds have planned for the afternoon?"

Lex looked at me, his gaze full of promise and fun. "I dunno. Abbie needs some photos for class, so I was thinking we'd meander around Notting Hill for a bit. Maybe head down to Oxford Street eventually and do some shopping."

I wrinkled my nose. I wasn't really in the mood for shopping. Especially with him. No need to fit into that gold digger stereotype. "Actually, Lex, why don't you hit the shops on your own? I might head to Hyde Park."

He just rolled his eyes. "Mother, have you ever met anyone who's allergic to shopping? Abbie refuses to go with me. And every time I drag her along, she spends the time taking pictures *outside* the shops. It's crazy." The ringing of his phone interrupted him. He looked down at his cell, then caressed my knuckles with his thumb. "I'm sorry, I have to take this."

While Lex took his call, his mother regaled me with stories of Alexi and Xander and their antics as young children. "Even then, though he's the younger one, Lex was so much more serious. If there was trouble, it was almost always Xander." A shadow crossed her beautiful features then flickered away just as quickly.

The sound of footsteps from the back of the house had me turning to see who was coming. A tall, imposing man with a confident stride walked in, clutching his phone in a death grip.

Stephanie stood quickly. "Abbie, meet my ex-husband, Reginald." To Alexi's dad she said, "I didn't expect to see you until much later. I don't have the papers ready for you to sign yet for the charity. Lex is just visiting with his girlfriend."

I studied the older man. It was easy to see where Alexi and Xander got their physical genes from. Their height, the broad shoulders, their lean, trim forms. They even inherited the silver-gray eyes of the older man. I suddenly wondered what it would be like to photograph all three of them together.

Although, the longer I studied the man, the more apparent it became that both Alexi and Xander got their smiles from their mother. Because this man did not smile. At all.

"Where is Alexi? I need to speak with him."

Stephanie's voice wavered slightly. "Reginald, don't be rude. You can at least say hello to Alexi's guest."

The older man turned his gaze on me, and I wanted to shrink into the furniture. The look of hatred on his face was enough to make me bristle. Alexi had said his father was unpleasant, but I hadn't expected something like this. *Fantastic.*

"You'll forgive me if I don't bother with Lex's dalliance of the moment. There are so many you see. I can't be bothered to learn all their names."

Stephanie Chase's face went bright red, then very pale. "Reginald, that is unacceptable. You apologize immediately."

I squirmed in my seat. I made an attempt at escape. "Uhm, I'll just go find Alexi and see what's keeping him. If you—"

The older man's sharp voice cut off my attempted escape. "You think you love my son? You'll soon realize he's not who

NANA MALONE

you think he is. He'll betray you, just like he's betrayed me. I had to find out today that he sold a software company right out from under me. If he'll do that to his own father, imagine what he'll do to you, a nobody."

Suddenly unable to breathe, I blinked rapidly to ward off impending tears. No wonder Alexi avoided his father. The man was toxic. "This seems like a family discussion, I'll—"

"No. My ex-wife wants me to play nice. Then let's have a chat about my son."

Stephanie put a hand on his arm. "Reginald, don't. Leave the poor girl be."

"You wanted me to play nice, I'm playing nice. I'm going to tell this young *lady*..." The gaze he slid over my body told me he considered me anything but. "...about my son."

Well, I certainly wasn't going to sit there while the asshole tore Alexi down in front of me. "With all due respect, Mr. Chase, I don't need to hear what you have to say about Alexi. I know him."

The older man's brows rose. "Then he's told you everything about himself?"

"We don't keep secrets from each other."

Reginald Chase laughed. Except the sound was cold and thin instead of rich, booming, and warm. "Is that so? Then you don't mind shacking up with a thief and a murderer who let his brother take the blame for a murder he committed?"

Everyone in the room froze. Stephanie stood with her mouth agape. Reginald's face was a mask of contorted fury, and out of the corner of my eye, I could see Alexi's stricken face as he stilled in the doorway.

No. No, no, no, no, no. I tried to swallow, tried desperately to breathe, but even my lungs were frozen. It was only when the room started to spin that I managed to drag in a breath.

It wasn't true. I'd just gotten caught up in some family dynamics that were frankly none of my business. The man Reginald was talking about... That wasn't Alexi. Except when I finally had the faculties to move my head and glance in his direction, he stared at me, a mask of horror and guilt stamped on his face.

Oh no. There had to be an explanation. It couldn't be. "Alexi, is this true?"

He shook his head, his eyes wide with horror and grief. "Abbie, I need you to listen to me for a minute."

I could see the truth in his eyes. But I didn't want to believe it. I needed the words. "Is it true?"

"Yes, but—"

I shook my head. "No. You've been keeping this from me."

"I tried to tell you. Then... I couldn't find the right time..." His voice trailed.

"No. When you have something important to tell someone, you just do. You don't lie to someone you care about."

"Abbie—" He reached for me.

"Alexi, don't." I shook my head trying to think. "I—I need to go."

With my shoulders back and my head held high, I strode out of the living room into the foyer. I took my coat from the hall closet.

As I slid it on, Alexi tried to hold my coat for me. "Let me help you."

I deliberately stepped out of his reach. "No, thank you. I have it." I didn't meet his gaze.

He ran his hands through his hair. "Abbie, don't do this. I can explain."

"Do what? Refuse to be lied to? You swore to me there was nothing else to tell me. And though I find it impossible to think you could ever hurt anyone, clearly, you're still hiding something. I'm not dealing with secrets or lies anymore, Alexi."

He reached for my hand. "Look, I'm coming with you. Just give me a minute. We can talk."

I tilted my head up to meet his gaze. "Alexi, I need you to tell me. We already covered this. No more secrets. No more lies. What is it you're hiding?"

His hands shook, and he shoved them into his pockets "Abbie, I'm sorry, I can't. I—"

I held up a hand even as I felt my heart tearing into pieces. There wasn't anything he could say that I wanted to hear. I tipped my chin up and leveled a stare at him. "I'm leaving."

CHAPTER TWENTY

LEX

After watching the woman I loved walk out of my life, I stalked back into the living room and rounded on my father. "Are you fucking happy now? She's gone. She won't ever be coming back. Thanks to you, I blew it."

My father glowered at me. "Don't you mean thanks to you? You're the one who shoved that nonce off the top of the stairs. You're the one who let Xander take the blame. And you're the one who didn't tell your little girlfriend."

Even as I balled my fists to strike the old man, my mother shouted from behind him, "That is enough, Reginald! You might be angry with Lex, but you had no right. He's your son. Don't you think he deserves some kind of happiness?"

My father's face turned first red, then purple. "My son? My fucking son? No son of mine would have sold a company that's rightfully mine out from under me. No son of mine would wait and let me find out by reading the fucking Times!"

I'd had enough. "You forget, old man, that you were the

one who pushed me into a corner. You've been threatening to cut off my trust fund ever since Uni. I had to make another way for myself. And I did. I don't need you or the fucking money."

"Stop being a spoiled brat, Alexi. Do you know how this makes me look in the industry? A multimillion-dollar deal like that, and it happened under my nose. You signed a non-compete like every other employee."

I chuckled mirthlessly. "What? You think that's not the first thing I thought of? I'm not a fool. Take Back the Night is in no way related to any of the software you build at CET. And I had my lawyer look over my non-compete specifically. It stated that I would not enter or engage in any business that is in direct conflict with the Chase technologies umbrella. CET has no lifestyle products, direct apps, or games that are in any way related to the entertainment space or sector. My non-compete also states that any and all documents or code authored by me is property of CET. Well, you'll be happy to know I didn't write a stitch of that code. Oh, I meticulously reviewed it, and it's my brainchild, but I didn't write it."

My father vibrated with anger. "You're a slippery git, aren't you?"

"Well this git just earned his freedom."

Reginald stepped into my space, and for the first time, I realized I'd edged out my father in height by an inch.

"You think this is over? You're still not touching that trust fund."

I merely shrugged. "The good news is I don't need it. I can actually work for myself doing something I love. And be paid handsomely. In case you hadn't heard, I'm rich. Not as rich as I would be, but honestly, I don't need much." I glanced at my mother, who'd gone pale. "Besides, you can't keep it from me forever. I have plans for that money. There's a youth center in Brixton that would be happy to have the funds."

In that moment, as my father glared at me, I saw how much the old man despised me.

"I knew I should have sent you off to school with your brother. I was a fool then to listen to your mother. After all, she was the reason there was a scandal to begin with."

My mother's gasp of shock made me contemplate beating the old man to a bloody pulp again. Grief tore through me as I said, "You leave her out of this. Don't you think you've done enough damage today without going after Mum too? Why can't you just care about our happiness? I love Abbie, and you did your level best to run her off." The admission tore through my chest and left me bereft. For several seconds, I wasn't sure I could breathe.

My father raised an eyebrow. "I'm talking about how your little deal has crippled my reputation, and you're talking about a girl?" He scowled. "I should have seen then what I see now. You're not worth it."

I glared at my father's retreating back as my mother sobbed quietly behind me. When I turned to face her, I tried to soften my voice. "Mum, are you okay?"

My mother's hands shook as she placed them over her heart. "Lex, I—I'm sorry. I didn't know he would come by now or how angry he would be. I would have warned you."

"How could you know? I knew he'd be pissed about the sale, but I never thought he'd say those things. Dredge up the past like that. I mean you should have seen the look on her face." I shoved a hand in my hair. Fear chased the disbelief. Then the dread settled in around me. Abbie was really gone. My heart squeezed. In the back of my mind I'd known this would happen when she found out. But I'd dared hope. After the dread came the panic. I wouldn't ever get to hold her again.

My mother's hands trembled as she reached for me. "Lex. Maybe we can fix this. Maybe if you told her what happened that night."

I shook my head with enough force to bring my hair onto my brow. "No. I lied to her, again. She has no reason to ever believe anything I say. I've fucking lost her." The hollow thud of my pulse drummed between my ears as my knees wobbled. I'd really lost her.

"This is all my fault." My mother paled and braced herself on the arm of the couch before she sank into it. "I was so selfish I couldn't see the devil and protect my own children. There isn't a day that goes by that I don't regret not protecting you enough. I wish I'd been the one to do it. I dream about it every day. I wish I could resurrect him just so I could have a mother's pleasure of tearing his wretched flesh from his bones. I would kill to protect you." Tears rolled down her face. "I would die to protect you."

I winced. I didn't need her reliving her guilt about what that asshole had tried to do to me and my brother. "No, Mum. This isn't your fault. I should have found a way to tell Abbie. I know she has trust issues. Dad's right. I'm the one who blew it."

My mother's dark brown eyes shimmered with tears. "You really do love her, don't you?"

"Yes. I do." But that didn't matter now.

❦

ABBIE

I rolled my shoulders as I trudged up the stairs to my flat. Through the door, I could hear Sophie and Faith laughing about something. I briefly considered going out somewhere so I wouldn't have to explain, but I was exhausted and just wanted my bed.

My hands shook as I thought of Alexi and what his father had said. I couldn't believe that he'd deliberately killed someone. He might be keeping things from me, but he wasn't a killer. I knew him well enough to know that. So, what the fuck was going on? What had happened?

When I opened the door, Faith gave me a cheery smile. "So how did it go with mummy? Does she love you as we all do?"

My glance skipped over her sunny, wholesome smile and landed on Sophie's concerned one. Mimicking Faith's accent, I said, "Mummy was lovely, but Daddy was a pill and sent me packing. He aired all the family's dirty laundry and said some horrible things about Alexi."

Sophie's face fell. "Abena, I'm so sorry. From what I've heard, his father is awful."

"That he is."

Faith looked back and forth between us. "So, what did the old geezer say exactly?"

I didn't know how much to share. Alexi might have lied to me, but his business was still his business. I didn't want to be the one to put him and his family in the crosshairs again. "Turns out, Lex is still lying. Protecting some family scandal."

Sophie's eyes went wide. "A scandal? Honey, that's what Google was invented for."

I winced. "I dunno. That feels somehow icky. I—"

Sophie handed me the laptop. "Look, you guys have been through enough. You can either get to the bottom of it, or you can let him go. Sooner or later, you have to make a choice. You've been looking for a reason to run from him. Any reason. And while lying is a legit reason to not be with someone, you haven't exactly been all in. You've been waiting for him to disappoint you like Easton did. And he's a different guy."

Faith shrugged. "I'm shocked to say it, but Sophie speaks sense."

Sophie swatted her with a pillow. "Shit, I hate that he makes you hurt, but maybe he hasn't told you everything because he knows you'll run."

I shook my head. "No, that's bullshit. He could tell me anything. I wouldn't judge him."

Sophie wrapped an arm around me. "But how is he supposed to know that? You've run from this thing the moment there was trouble."

"I'm not running. I'm just... thinking."

Faith tapped the laptop. "Well, think fast. Because you seem happy with him. The faster you guys work out your issues, the sooner you get to the making-up portion of the fight. And I want a play by play."

Sophie laughed, and I turned on the laptop. Alexi wasn't Easton. I knew that. Alexi had always taken care of me. Treated me like I was special. Taken his time with me. The girls were right. If I wanted him, I needed to trust him. Which meant finding out what he was trying so hard to keep buried. But I wasn't going to dig it up. I didn't want some bullshit spun story on the Internet. I wanted him to tell me. I wanted him to trust me. But what would I do if he wouldn't? Could I walk away from him?

CHAPTER TWENTY-ONE

LEX

I turned off the video of the interview I'd done with BBC One that would air tomorrow. In less than twenty-four hours, I'd be a multimillionaire. All on my own, without a dime of my father's money. Toshino had given some leeway on the press, as it was about my personal life and Toshino Inc hadn't been mentioned.

I had no one to share it with. Not that Nick hadn't already called to gloat over how good we looked on television. But the person I wanted to share it with was Abbie. But I'd ruined that. She wasn't coming back.

When my doorbell rang, I checked the time. Ten thirty. It was far too late for a delivery. I'd just talked to Nick, so maybe it was Gemma needing someplace to crash. When I opened the door, my heart seized. Abbie stood on the threshold, sopping wet under her leaking umbrella.

Automatically, I held out a hand and helped her onto the barge. "Abbie, what—"

She put up her hands. "Wait, before you say anything. I

have to say I'm sorry I ran. I couldn't take the secrets, and I ran. I have no idea how to trust anymore." Her tears mingled with the rain drops and streaked down her face. "I'm so sorry. I should have just stayed and listened, but I was scared that I was stepping back into an old pattern of accepting lies. I—I shouldn't have run. I always run. I don't want to run anymore."

I watched her expressive face as she cried and explained and babbled. Her eyes widened, and she nervously licked at her lips with the tip of her tongue. She rubbed at her temples like she always did when she was having a full-scale melt-down, and I loved her.

She'd chased *me* down. She'd recognized the pattern, and she'd broken it all on her own. She'd come back to me. Without thought, I pulled her to me and kissed her, cutting off her stream of consciousness. With her still-dripping umbrella and her soaked-through coat and rain dripping off the ends of her braids, I kissed her with all the pent-up frustration and shame and love I had. I loved her. More than I deserved to, more than I dared to, but I loved her.

And regardless of what my father had said, she'd come back for me.

My hands shook. "I didn't think I'd be seeing you again."

"I need the truth, Alexi. I don't want us to keep doing this. Please. Can you tell me?"

A harsh chuckle ripped out of me. "I've been so worried I was going to lose you when you found out, I ended up pushing you away by hiding the truth."

"Your father didn't run me off with what he said about you. The only reason I ran is because I couldn't stand you lying to me, hiding things from me. Nothing you've done can scare me off as long as I know that you're open with me."

I trembled. *No, it's not true. She'll leave, and when she does, it'll break you.* No. I wasn't going to lose her. Not for anything.

"Mum and Dad split up when I was about three or four. She started seeing someone else a couple of years later. At first, Silas was the television dad you see. Played games with us. Took us to the park for a bit of football, that sort of thing. You've met my father. Even then, he wasn't particularly warm."

I ran a hand through my hair. I was desperate to get it all out so there wouldn't be anything left hanging between us. "Everything changed when he asked Mum to marry him. Xan and I were ecstatic. We thought we were finally getting a real father. Someone to love us. But that's not what we got."

I shivered as my memories weaved into the forefront of my mind. "Mum started working more international charities and traveling more, leaving us with the nannies and Silas." My voice broke, and I loathed the weakness that I heard in myself. "She didn't know that he used to sneak into mine and Xan's bedroom at night and put his hands on us. When we fought back, he beat us. Never anywhere visible. He was apparently too smart for that."

Abbie gasped and whispered, "Oh, God."

"We had five different nannies in the fourteen months he was with my mother, each of them too scared to help two little boys who couldn't help themselves."

"Alexi—"

"No, Abbie, you need to hear it all. One night, while my

mother worked downstairs, he snuck into our room. Xander ran away from him, and he was going after him to make sure he didn't find the nanny or Mum. I knew if he caught Xander, it would mean another beating. I didn't want him to hurt us anymore. I couldn't take it. So I ran after him. When he caught hold of Xander's T-shirt, I only wanted to get him off my brother. I—" My voice shook. I prayed that I could stop the pain, but I had to get it all out first. "We were at the top of the stairs, and I pushed him. *Hard.* With everything I had, I pushed him. I wanted him dead."

Her voice was whisper soft. "Oh, Alexi."

"And Dad was right. Even at six, I understood that what I'd done was horrific. I understood what I was. I knew they'd send me away, but I didn't care." I sniffed and wiped at my nose. "But instead they sent Xander away. We told them it was an accident, that we'd heard him fall, but the way he protected me, they assumed he'd done it. He made me promise I'd never tell. He just stepped right in front of me and shielded—" My voice shook. "And I let him."

Abbie placed both palms on my chest. "Enough, that's enough. I don't need to hear any more. I'm so sorry."

I couldn't meet her gaze. "I don't know how you can stand to look at me. My own father can't. I tried to talk to him then. He blamed us. We tried to make him understand, but as far as he was concerned, we'd tarnished the family name with the scandal of it all."

"You were a child, protecting your brother. They were the adults. They were supposed to protect you. It was your mother and father's job to protect you. None of what happened was your fault."

"Mum didn't know. I think after it happened, when they sent Xan to a string of therapists, she suspected, but she didn't know the kind of man she was about to marry. She would have killed him. Dad, well, after the fact, he covered everything up. Xan was sent to boarding school, and I'm pretty sure Dad looked into Silas's background. He was so careful, but he'd probably done something like that before." I dragged in a shaky breath. "Xan and I never stood a chance. We're completely fucked up."

She placed a hand on my cheek. "Stop. You've grown into an incredible man who's kind and loyal and smart. Don't let those shadows take any of what you've become away from you. I will help chase them off."

I blinked rapidly as emotion overwhelmed me. She really wasn't running from me. I dared to hope, dared to hold on to the thread that she was mine. "You really don't hate me?"

"No, Alexi. I'm going to keep telling you how much I love you until it finally sinks in."

Desperation dripped from each word as I held her close. "I thought I'd lost you for good."

She clung to me, her hands threading through my hair. "I'm so sorry. I should have trusted you."

"I didn't think you would still want me after what he said to you."

"Yes." She kissed me softly, her full lips feeling like heaven against mine. "I still want you. I've wanted you since you saved me from death by Mini Cooper. I wanted you that first time we danced. I wanted you at your party. I wanted you when you showed up on my doorstep. Even when the paparazzi were camped out on my lawn and making me miserable, I still wanted you. There is nothing your father could say to me to make me not want you. There's nothing you can do to make me not want you. There's nothing in your past that can scare me off." She shivered in my arms.

I crushed her to my chest, unwilling to let her go. "Abbie, I love you. I'm not even sure when I started falling in love with you. Maybe it was Brixton. Maybe it was the first time I saw you sitting in that massive puddle drenched and trying to save your camera instead of yourself."

"I love you."

The glowing warmth spread from my chest and started to thaw the icicles. But I frowned. She couldn't possibly love me if she knew what had happened. What I'd done. "Abbie, I—"

She pressed her fingers against my lips. "Shh. Did you really think that I wouldn't love you? That it would matter to me? You were a child when it all happened, and you've been carrying that guilt all on your own for years when you had nothing to feel guilty for."

She pushed the braids out of her face. Just having her close made the blood rush in my ears, and I wanted to kiss her. She licked her lips, and I bit back a moan.

As if sensing the change in me, she whispered, "Alexi."

"Shh, let me get you out of these wet things."

First, I slid her sodden coat off her shoulders and let it fall to the floor. She followed suit and toed off her wool-lined boots. Right there, I peeled off the rest of her wet clothing and carried her naked, lithe form to my bedroom.

I swallowed around the lump in my throat as I drank in every inch of her soft flesh. I knew how she tasted, how she felt in every nook of her body. I knew her heart. Knew her fears. It was the first time I'd ever let myself know anyone. Let anyone know me. And it felt liberating. And terrifying. And right. "I love you, Abena."

She pressed her body into me, and every nerve ending howled to be inside her, to fit our bodies together and drive into her until we both found peaceful oblivion. I gently tucked her into my bed, then stripped off my clothes.

Unmistakable heat flashed in her eyes, and I couldn't help a quick grin. Sliding in beside her, I tucked her against me so that we spooned with my hand cupping her breast.

"Lex, what—"

"I'm going to hold you, if that's okay. You know how much I want you." I dragged in a sharp breath. "Hell, you can feel it." My cock twitched against the soft globes of her ass. I paused and kissed her shoulder, gritting my teeth against the onslaught of lust as the satin skin of her backside wiggled against me. "But I need to hold you more than I need to make love to you."

She nodded and tucked her face into my arm. "I heard from my sister."

I kissed the nape of her neck. "Hmmm?"

"She said Easton went to see my family with his new girlfriend."

I cursed under my breath. "Jesus, that poor woman."

I nodded. "He said he'd tried to talk sense into me and I overreacted. My mother actually thanked him. If you can believe that."

"God, sweetheart, I'm so sorry."

"It's fine. I don't need her to believe in me. She's my

mother. I love her. But I don't have to like her or put up with her when she's giving me bullshit."

"I'm really proud of you."

"Yeah well, it's taken a long time to get here." She nuzzled in. "Oh, he did mention that he'd seen where I'd been spending my time. And the kind of boyfriend I had who lived on a boat in squalor."

I sniffed, indignant. "I mean, this barge has less square footage than Killian's three thousand square feet, but I take offense at that. I suppose I need to buy you something bigger now."

She laughed. "No thank you. This place is ridiculous, and you know it. I'm so sorry he wrecked this place. I know you don't blame me, but I'm indirectly responsible."

"One day, I hope you don't believe that anymore."

"I'm getting closer every day."

It took me an hour before I was able to fall asleep, but I hadn't been that at peace in longer than I could remember.

ABBIE

I moaned into Lex's chest. I was awake enough to know I was having either the very best of dreams or one hell of a wakeup call. Lex kissed me as his thumb and forefinger rolled one of my nipples. Sighing into the caress, I let myself relax into his kiss. His expert tongue caressed and teased mine into playing.

God, I relished what he could do to my body. The way he made me pliant. He never rushed me, even when I wanted to hurry. He always took his time with everything, even kissing me, like we had all the time in the world. Like his erection wasn't straining.

I loved kissing him. His lips were so soft and skilled and his tongue–every time he licked into my mouth, it made me shiver. When his hand dipped between my thighs, I parted them to ease his way. Skilled fingers stroked my cleft, teasing me, driving me crazy. I arched my back trying to angle my hips into his hand.

Alexi slid a finger inside me as his thumb caressed my clit, and I cried out and sank my fingers into his hair. He grunted in satisfaction as my hips bucked, then he sucked on my tongue in time with his fingers sliding into my slick center. His heavy erection continued to press into my thigh, and I moaned. I would never get over what he could do to my body. I'd never been so carnal, so aroused, so willing to give myself completely to anyone.

With a groan, he pulled back from our kiss, and I mewled as I tried to follow his lips. His gaze scorched me. Dark and fiery, he stared at me under hooded lids. "Jesus, what are you doing to me?"

My constricted throat made it impossible to speak, so I responded the only way I knew how–by arching my hips into his hand again.

He muttered a soft curse, and squeezed his eyes shut. As his fingers strummed me to the edge of orgasm, he chewed on his bottom lip. When he increased the pace of his questing fingers, I held tight onto his shoulders. I rotated my hips around and around until he swore again and rubbed his thumb directly over my clit.

My orgasm ripped through me, laying destruction to every nerve and cell. Unable to think, I threw my head back, giving myself over fully to the sensation.

"Holy, fuck, you are so beautiful when you come."

Still unable to speak, I dragged in ragged breaths. If I hadn't been fully awake earlier, I certainly was now. "That was a hell of a wakeup call."

He slowly withdrew his fingers from me. "I'm not done yet."

I smiled up at him, expecting him to go for a condom, but instead, he burrowed under the covers. His hands parting my thighs had me tensing. "Lex, wait, I–"

He drew back the covers so he could look at me. "I should have asked you last time. Is this something you don't like?"

Oh God, he looked so concerned and worried about me. How the hell was I supposed to tell him? Embarrassment made my skin hot and flushed. "Before you, I–I've never done it. Or rather, I guess no one has done it to me before."

His brows snapped down "You're kidding me, right?"

I bit my lip as I shook my head. "N-no. I, ah, Ea—uhm— no one's ever wanted to." I turned my face into the pillow too embarrassed to continue. God, I should have just kept my mouth shut. Now he thought I was some kind of freak.

With strong fingers, he turned my chin so I was looking at him. His gaze burned hot, and the desire etched on his face was unmistakable. "Tasting you is so arousing for me. I love how you taste. But only if you're comfortable."

"I—uh..." Wow, he wanted to? I nodded emphatically. "Yes. I'm comfortable."

"Oh, thank God." His smile was lopsided. "I think I'd die if I couldn't taste you."

He slid back down my body, placing kisses across my chest and belly as he went. When he reached my hips, he nibbled at the flesh on my pelvic bone then scooted lower.

Dusting feather light kisses on my inner thighs, he paused when he got to my cleft. "So pretty. And so soft." His first stroke of my slick center had me clenching my hands into the sheets. Oh God. He lapped at me, kissing me and exploring me with his tongue. He took his time like with everything else. He seemed in no hurry. When his tongue circled the throbbing bundle of nerves, I flew apart in his hands again. A little embarrassed, I tried to drag him back up my body by tugging on his hair, but he didn't let up. He kept stroking me. Kept lapping at me.

It wasn't until he slid a finger into my moist sheath again that I lost all my inhibitions. If he was intent on killing me with ecstasy, then who the hell was I to argue? Finally relaxing, I let my thighs fall apart and he moaned, parting my folds and dipping the tip of his finger into my center. My third orgasm rolled through me, chasing the tail of the previous one, and he didn't let up until I lay limp.

He drew himself back up my body, pausing to nip at my hips again, then to suckle my breasts.

When he made it to my lips, he asked, "I hope you'll let me taste you often."

I shivered. He could do that to me any time he wanted. "God, yes. I don't even know what to say."

"How about saying you'll let me taste you as often as I want."

I giggled. "Be my guest."

He shifted against my parting thighs with his, and I moaned when the tip of his erection nudged my cleft.

He squeezed his eyes shut tight as he entered me inch by inch. I met him halfway by raising my hips. His jaw stayed tight until he was seated all the way inside me. He made love to me sweetly. Kissing me, holding me to him, and looking into my eyes. "I love you Abena Nartey. I will never stop."

In that moment, the fear fell away. This was the perfect moment I'd always looked for. This was the kind of love and acceptance I'd been looking for all my life. "I love you too. Blissful abandon started in my toes and cascaded through my body. I held onto him tight and muttered how much I loved him as the orgasm took over all my conscious and subconscious thought.

As my body held him inside me, he whispered in my ear, "I am so lucky." With two more deep strokes, his whole body shook with release.

CHAPTER TWENTY-TWO

ABBIE

I woke up parched.

When Alexi said he wasn't going to let me sleep, I thought that was a euphemism.

But I was exhausted, completely replete. And I was happy. I knew I was loved. I knew that even when something terrifying happened, I was going to be okay. I knew I was strong enough to stand on my own, but I didn't have to.

Also, I was pretty sure I couldn't walk straight. The man could pretty much go all damn night.

I threw off the covers and winced as I throbbed between my thighs. Jesus Christ, he really hadn't taken it easy on me. But it was a good pain. The kind of sore that I was willing to feel for the rest of my life.

I reached around, looking for something to wear to stave off the chill on the boat. When I found his discarded t-shirt, I picked it up and slid it over my head, relishing the soft fabric sliding over my skin.

Barefoot, I bypassed the shower where Alexi was singing

to himself and then padded down the cool hardwood out to the living space. Alexi must have pulled down the blackout shades on the barge because there was no light coming into the living room. The only illumination came from the kitchen.

I let the moonlight guide me. It took me three tries looking in the cabinets to find where he kept the glasses or mugs. When I found one, I searched around for the kettle and set that on as well.

When the water boiled, I poured two cups and dropped in the tea bags, adding sugar to mine and honey to his.

There was a sound behind me in the kitchen, and I smiled to myself. "I am exhausted. I couldn't possibly do any of that again," I teased. "I mean unless you were to kiss my neck again, and when you're kissing my neck, I can pretty much be talked into anything."

"That's good to know."

I whipped around. It was not Alexi. Even with the moonlight, it was hard to see who I was looking at. "Who's there?"

A man stepped from the shadows. Not as tall as Alexi, but broader, he menacingly stalked toward me. "This is your fault. My life is ruined because of you."

I tried to back up, but I just hit the stove. "Please, don't."

As he came closer, I could see that he was older, graying at the temples, and there were some lines around his eyes. "Who are you?"

"For years, I bided my time, waited for my opportunity. And when that finally comes, my chance to shape a dynasty, he won't cooperate, the ungrateful piece of shit."

I reached my hands behind me, trying to be careful of the

cook top as I tried to reach the handle of the teapot. "I don't understand."

"I have done nothing but serve this family to the best of my ability. But then you came along, and suddenly, the prince is acting reckless. He's taking risks. He's forgetting what we worked so hard for. All for you."

Who was this? I had no idea what he was talking about. "Do you know Alexi?"

"Do I know Alexi? I've only been standing here in the shadows guiding his future for his entire life. Everything was going well until you turned up. You have ruined everything that I have worked for. He met you and no longer cared. He could no longer be controlled."

I shook my head. "I don't understand what you mean. Why don't we wait for Alexi to come out of the shower, and we'll all talk about this?"

He raised his hand. It was then that I saw the gun.

"Oh my God!"

"No, we will not be waiting for Alexi. You just have to vanish. With you gone, everything will go back to the way it's supposed to be."

"Look, I don't know what's going on, but maybe we could just talk about this."

"There'll be no talking." I winced as he shouted.

"Okay, we don't—we don't have to talk. But I don't understand how I ruined everything. I'll just go. I'll go. It's fine. I will un-ruin everything." The hell I was going, but I needed to distract him so I wouldn't be trapped in there.

"You think I'm an idiot? You traipsed in with your magic twat, and you ruined my only shot at the throne."

I frowned. "You want Alexi on the throne?"

"Yes, the fucking throne. Everyone knows Xander is useless. He'll make the worst choice for king ever. Alexi was the choice. But you've tainted him. The public has seen you with him, seen his poor choices. Do you think they'll ever accept someone like you? You're nothing but a whore. His black—"

Alexi interrupted. "If I were you, I'd choose my next fucking words wisely."

ALEXI...

I'd heard Abbie's voice from the loo. I'd come out to convince her to get back into bed and let me take care of her... with my tongue.

Instead, I found her in the kitchen, terrified for her life.

I glared at Jean Claude. "What the fuck are you doing here, Jean Claude?"

He turned slowly, the light from the pier illuminating his face. When I'd stalked through the living room, I'd lifted the blinds so it wouldn't be nearly as dark. I'd also called the police, and I really hoped they'd fucking hurry.

"You want to know what I'm doing here? I'm doing what has to be done."

I swallowed hard, my gaze clashing with Abbie's. She was scared, backed up against the stove, cowering. My guts twisted. Because of me, she looked like that. Because of me, someone had terrified her.

"It's you and I that have a problem. And we can talk about this."

Jean Claude shook his head. "No, no, we cannot. I tried talking to you, but you wouldn't listen, insisting your heart knew what it wanted. But you don't understand. You've ruined everything. Do you think they'll accept her? She's black, for the love of Christ. African, to boot. If she'd been famous or wealthy in her own right, I could have spun that. I could have made that happen. But no. You found someone whose parents have no aspirations to greatness. A couple of attorneys are hardly worth noting. You couldn't go find a black princess... No, you had to go and find a black commoner. I can't make that work. You've ruined everything. The public has seen you traipsing around with her. I cannot save you unless she's gone."

I ran my hand through my hair. "Okay, Jean Claude, I hear you. I understand. But you don't have to do this. We still have a viable option with Xander."

The things I was saying made my stomach turn, but I had to keep him talking and keep him the fuck away from Abbie.

"Why don't you follow me, we'll have a drink."

"I'm not falling for that. Until we get rid of her, there is no hope. And everything I worked my whole life for is over unless she's gone."

I refused to look at Abbie, refused to even give him an opening. "Okay, I hear you. Fine. Let's just send her back to America. We'll say she broke my heart. You could make it work. You can make anything work. In this game, you are the best. Everyone knows it."

For a moment, I thought maybe he believed me. Maybe

he was buying it. But then he started to turn toward Abbie. "No, Jean Claude, look at me."

"You're just trying to protect her. You think I don't know what you're doing? No, she has to die. If she dies, the public will have sympathy for you. They'll see your poor suffering soul, and they'll want to ease it. And then you'll make an excellent prospect as a king."

"I'm not even a prospect, Jean Claude. My cousin sits on the throne."

"Not for long. All you have to do is wait and not make any errors or mistakes. All you have to do is be patient. But you can't be with this whore."

I clenched my teeth but said nothing. I had to get him out of there. Out of the kitchen.

Slowly, I started to back out. "Just come with me, Jean Claude. We'll talk about this. I understand what you're saying. I never saw it your way before." He started to take a step toward me, and I thought we were home free. But then I heard the click. Was that the safety? "Jean Claude—"

Apparently, Abbie didn't plan on going anywhere. She grabbed the kettle and swung it wildly, smacking him in the head.

He howled, and she launched herself, managing to scoot past him. Then she was running and darting for me.

I took her hand and tugged her forward. "Get in the closet, at the door."

"No, I'm not leaving you."

"You have to go."

She shook her head, so I did the only thing I could. I

opened the closet and shoved her in. I knew that the door handle was fidgety. She'd never get it open from the inside.

I hated doing that to her, but it was the only way to keep her safe. When I turned around, Jean Claude sauntered into the living room.

"Alexi," Jean Claude called. "Give her to me. This will all go away. Everything will be fine if you just give her to me."

"I'm sorry. I can't, Jean Claude. I know that you're trying to protect me, the family. I understand. But this isn't the way. Killing her isn't necessary. Nothing good will come of that."

"What do you know? Give her to me." He advanced on me, not raising the gun, but I knew he wouldn't hesitate to shoot Abbie.

I stepped forward. "No, we're not doing this, Jean Claude. Enough is enough. The police are already on their way."

He squinted his gaze at me. "You are really making this choice. This woman over your family?"

"Yeah. You don't get it. She *is* my family."

"Will she still be your family if she knows everything?"

"As a matter of fact, she *does* know everything. It took me a while to tell her because I was an idiot. But I did, and she accepts me. You're not ruining this."

I couldn't have foreseen what he was going to do next.

After all, everything he'd ever done had been to protect us, me and Xan. He'd been the one to handle the media after Silas McMahon's death. He'd been the one to find our therapist and the one looking after us from the shadows. But what he wanted to do now, that wasn't looking after us. That was pure self-interest. I never expected him to attempt to hit me.

I ducked his wild swing easily and then popped him in the face. He tossed the gun and then roared and charged me.

"Jean Claude, stop it. This isn't what you want." But he knew what he wanted. He charged right at my center, slamming me back against the wall.

The pain in my back had me wincing, but I quickly brought my elbows down on the back of his neck, landing three hard shots before he finally backed off, staggering.

Outside, I could hear the sirens. And then there was chatter and running footsteps. The police had arrived. But he had his hands on my collar and he was tugging me forward.

I landed a fist, but he didn't let go. He tossed me down and delivered a sharp, swift kick to my chest.

I rolled on the ground and coughed. I saw what he was doing. He was going for the closet. *Shit. Abbie.*

I forced myself to a sitting position and pushed my hands against the floor, propelling myself to my feet.

I grabbed him by the back of his shirt and pulled hard. I heard the rip, but I didn't care. As long as I kept him away from her.

When I dragged him back, I tossed him to the ground. All I knew was that I had to protect her, and I would do anything to make that happen.

My first fist landed on his nose, and blood spurted everywhere.

The next fist did more of the same, and I kept delivering blows, even through the shouting and knocking at the door. He wanted to kill Abbie, and I had to stop him. I finally went into the zone where I couldn't hear anything, where it was deadly silent and all that mattered was that my fists connected.

Abbie's voice was what finally broke through the haze. "Alexi, stop. Alexi, you don't want to do this. I'm okay. Everything is okay, but you have to stop."

My fist was raised, and I could feel the blood leaking between my knuckles, making the slide of my fingers against each other squishy like a trainer walking in mud. But her voice soothed me. "You don't want to do this. That's not who you are. Let him go."

I glared down at him. His face was barely recognizable, one eye swollen shut, his lips busted and bleeding, a tooth knocked out. There was blood everywhere. I frowned and pushed up and away from him, staggering to the door to let in the police. When I did, there was a rush of activity, bodies flooding my barge. I had to battle the stream of them just to reach her. And when I finally did, she wrapped her arms around me. "Thank you for saving me."

"Thank you, for saving me."

I kissed the top of her head and held her close. The ambulance was there with the police. It was all over. I was finally free to be with her. And I wasn't going to let anything stop that from happening.

CHAPTER TWENTY-THREE

ABBIE

Three days later.

Contentedly, I sipped my tea and watched Alexi cook...
shirtless. I could really get used to this. He'd brought
me to the beach to get away from it all. An overnight trip had
turned into three blissful days of uninterrupted together
time.

I'd put everything on hold just to be with him. Xander
hadn't been thrilled that I'd missed our weekly meeting, but it
was so worth it. Alexi's one conversation with his brother had
been short and brief, but he looked more relaxed after they'd
spoken. A few days with Alexi alone was just what I needed.
What we both needed.

It hadn't come free though. Now I'd have to rush to
complete my next assignment. And I had a make-up meeting
scheduled for that afternoon with Xander. No doubt I'd get
an earful about responsibility and squandering opportunities,
but I didn't really care.

Alexi looked up from the sausages. "What's that smile on your face for?"

I shrugged. "Oh nothing. Just admiring the view."

He smirked and turned the sausages. "You know, one of these days, we're going to have to get you to do some shirtless cooking."

"You wish. Besides, that would prove dangerous for me. I have a lot more wobbly bits than you do. Cooking can be hazardous to my health. I think I'll leave it to you."

"I promise you, if you were cooking naked, you wouldn't even make it to the stove before I dragged you back to bed."

"I can live with that." My phone vibrated on the tabletop. I glanced at the incoming text message.

Xander: *Meet me in the labs at one sharp. We need to discuss program demands.*

Alexi gave me a soft smile. "Duty calls?"

"Yeah, just a reminder that I need to return to real life."

He nodded. "Me too. I wish we could stay longer."

"Tell me about it. But we have each other. Somehow it makes the big, bad, scary world more tolerable."

He grinned as he served my plate. "That it does."

ABBIE

When I got to the labs, I was surprised to find Xander developing prints of some of my work. "I see you got the photos I sent from my last shoot with Jasper."

He nodded. "Yeah, I figured I'd go old school with some of them."

I shifted uncomfortably from foot to foot as Xander examined my photos. He pointed to one of the ones I'd done with Angel's model friends. "Is that Serena Winchell?"

I blinked rapidly. Was I going to get into trouble for using an actual model? My stomach rolled. "Yes, she's sort of a friend of a friend."

"I worked with her in Milan. For someone so young, she has an ethereal quality to her. And a good work ethic."

I blinked in surprise. "She was great. Didn't complain once, no matter how long it took me to set up a shot."

Xander nodded then smirked. "She's fantastic in the sack, too."

My gaze shifted up from the photo to stare at Xander. Had he just said— "I beg your pardon?"

His laugh was low and mellow. A lot like Alexi's. He probably drove every woman he worked with mad with that laugh. "I just wanted to see what you'd say."

I raised a brow. "So, she's *not* good in the sack? Poor thing, I hope you didn't tell her that. The girl will have a complex for life."

He stared at me a long moment before a deep, bellowing laugh broke free from his chest. "You surprise me Abbie. You think fast on your feet, and you're not unsettled by me."

"Well, not as much anymore. But you still are my teacher."

His voice was soft when he spoke. "Not for long."

Oh hell. He hated these photos, too? "Look, I've worked my ass off. You can't cut me from the program. You have no idea what I had to do to get the money for my next semester. Just give me another chance."

Frown lines furrowed his brow. "Why the hell do you think I'm cutting you from the program?"

Wait. What? "That bad week I had. You said if I ever took another set of shitty photos you'd cut me. I did my best on this shoot. I—"

He put up his hands and interrupted me. "Hey, stop. I'm not cutting you. I was a bit hard on you that day. Yes, I wanted you to bring me your A game, but admittedly I was a little jealous and thought you were distracted by my brother."

I narrowed my eyes. "So, what? You were scaring me straight?"

He shrugged. "Something like that. I would never cut you. You're extraordinarily talented. Not to mention beautiful."

All I could do was shake my head at him. Well he'd accomplished his goal. I had been terrified of losing my spot. "Are you always such a pain in the ass?"

He laughed then studied me for a minute. "You don't seem fazed by me anymore."

"I'm not going to deny that you're pretty to look at, but I'm not interested. And I'm still your student."

He grinned at me. "And you stand up for yourself when someone's being an ass."

"Yes, I do." I frowned. "You might be my teacher, but if you're being a wanker, I'll call you on it." I tried not to wince at my Americanization of the word *wanker*. It just didn't sound as cool as when Faith and Sophie said it.

"It's been a while since someone called me a wanker to my face."

I bit my tongue. He still had the power to fail me in is

hands, and I needed a recommendation. "Sometimes my mouth runs away with me." That was all I was willing to concede in the way of an apology.

"That's not a bad thing. I'm looking for someone who can put me in my place, not be rattled by straight talk or sex talk or cursing. And someone with incredible talent."

What? He was auditioning bed partners? "Look, Xander, as intriguing as your offer is, I have to tell you I have a boyfriend, and considering he's your brother, I think what you're asking is inappropriate."

His brows drew down, "So you don't want to work for me then?"

I barely heard him as I continued. "I mean, it's not fair to proposition your students, we depend on you for our—" My brain halted then sputtered to life again as what he'd said settled in. "You want me to come work for you?"

His arrogant smirk slid back into place. "Well, that was until you mentioned propositioning. If I have a choice, I'll take propositioning."

My face flamed, and I ducked my head. "Shit, sorry about that. It just sounded like you were offering me a job as your mistress or something, not your assistant."

He laughed. "You can relax. I know what you mean to Lex. And while I am a womanizing manwhore, I also work my ass off, and I could use an assistant with your talent. It's technically a work-study position. The official assistant job won't be available until the course ends, but as long as you don't screw up, it's as good as yours."

Elation and joy skipped over my synapses. "I don't even know what to say."

"How about you say yes and put me out of my misery."

My body vibrated with giddy excitement. "You're sure you want me? I mean I don't have a lot of experience, and I could use some work in some areas and—"

He held up a hand, and his dark eyes met my gaze. "I'm positive. You're the one with the most talent in the class. Even when you're not at your best, you're still better than most professionals I've seen. You earned it."

I grinned and spun around in a happy little twirl. He grinned back. "Wait, can I still do my side gigs? I know assistant jobs don't pay much."

"Yes. As long as they don't interfere with your work for me. But I should have mentioned the work-study position covers half your tuition."

I squealed again. *Half my tuition?* That meant I had enough money saved so far to pay for next semester as well. I did another happy twirl. "I have no idea what to say or do right now."

"Why don't you get out of here? I'll have my personal assistant call you with the details."

Tears threatened to spill over, and I rapidly blinked my eyes. "Thank you. Thank you. So much, thank you."

"Go on. Get out of here before I forget that you're my assistant and that I promised my brother I'd keep my hands and sexual innuendos to myself."

I skipped out of Xander's office and down the stairs of the Arts building. I was running so fast I squealed when someone snagged the back of my jacket. I whirled around, ready for a fight, only to see Alexi's grinning face.

"Easy there, tiger, where's the fire? In a hurry to get to

your boyfriend?"

I beamed. "Yes, actually. I have good news to share with him."

Snowflakes clung to his hair and his lashes and the tip of his nose. He looped his arms around my waist before pulling me in for a kiss. With his lips and tongue, he coaxed his way into my mouth, sliding his tongue against mine. He drugged me with his kiss, so my brain didn't have a hope of functioning properly. When he pulled back, his eyes were stormy with desire. "So, what is this good news you have to share?"

"Xander just offered me a position as his assistant."

Alexi grinned then squeezed me so hard I could hardly breathe.

"From the joyful expression on your face, I assume you said yes."

"You know, I never would have been able to do this without you." Unease tripped up my spine. Had he stepped in as my white knight even after I told him not to? "Wait, was this all your doing?"

He shook his head. "Xander came to me and asked my permission. He wanted to make sure I'd be okay with the two of you working together, but it was all him. This time I get to just be the happy boyfriend."

"I have never been so happy in my life, Alexi."

"Well, good thing for you, I only plan on building on this happy buzz you have going."

I laughed as he nuzzled my throat. "And just what are these plans of yours?"

"How about we start with us loving each other?"

I grinned up at him. "Done."

EPILOGUE

ALEXI

Present Day

We were ushered from the gallery quickly. Matthias and his fiancée wasted no time. Without preamble, Xander, myself, and Abbie were shoved into the waiting limousine.

I let Abbie go in first, and then my brother. Mathias went for the SUV on the street. Blake Security was already on the case. They knew how volatile this situation could get, and they were ready. Once we had a security firm on retainer in London, they'd pull out.

When I climbed in and the door closed, we pulled away from the curb. Xander ran both hands down his face. "Right. So, this is the new normal?"

My mother nodded slowly. "I'm sorry, both of you. But right now it's the safest thing. Until someone new is coronated with a clear successor, there will be those who might come for us in an attempt to gain the throne."

"Mother, I think they've already accomplished that. They're already coming for us," Xander muttered.

She shook her head. "I had hoped that Jean Claude was wrong, that none of this would ever come to fruition. But now that the day is here, I can't say that I'm going to turn it away."

I frowned. "Still feels too soon to mention that nutter's name."

She flushed and sent a soft smile Abbie's way. "I'm sorry to bring up painful memories. Just know that I don't wish he was back at all."

Abbie shook her head. "Forget it. Alexi is being too sensitive. I mean honestly. No one has tried to kill me in at least five years. You think he'd let it go already."

Even Abbie's humor couldn't lift my mood. I watched my mother. What did she want? How did she see this going forward? There was tension around her mouth and in her gaze. "Mum, what do you want us to do?"

"Well, I certainly don't want anyone to be in danger."

Xander chuckled darkly. "Well, it's a little too late for that. Can we just get back to the house so I can make sure Imani is okay?"

Xander's wife, Imani, was pregnant and sicker than a dog with morning sickness, so she'd opted not to come to the gallery opening.

When we reached my mother's house, there was already security in place. Blake Security was present as we all flowed into the living room.

Imani sat up and turned off Netflix. "Why is everyone home so early? Did you sell every piece?"

Abbie gave her a soft smile. "Um, I'm not sure."

Imani frowned. "What? Xander, what's going on?"

His gaze skittered to me and then to my mother. "Sweetheart, are you feeling all right?"

"Stop. Right now, I feel fine, but I would kill for a scone. Tell me what's going on."

He went and joined her on the couch and wrapped an arm around her. "Listen, something has happened. Mum's cousin, the King of Nomea, has been assassinated."

Imani's eyes went wide. "Shit," But one of the reasons she was so good for my brother was that she was steady, with both feet set firmly on the ground. She just got on with it. "What do we need to do?"

My mother sighed. "We have to make some decisions boys."

I took Abbie's hand and dragged her to my side. "Mum, we can't make any decisions right now. Can we? I mean, it all boils down to what *you* want to do."

"And that's the thing. I never asked for this, darling. But if it's mine by right, I think I should take it."

Xander, ever self-interested, asked the question I didn't want to. "So, what does that mean for us?"

"Well, officially, if I take the throne, you'll be princes of Nomea."

I sighed and cast my glance down to Abbie. When she spoke, her voice was soft. "What do you want, Alexi?"

"What I want is for nothing to change for us. You've already been through too much. Everything we went through to be together, and then Jean Claude trying to kill you for this very thing. This *throne*."

She cast her gaze down. "He was sick, obviously."

"Yeah, he was. But there will be a million more just like him. I'm not subjecting you to that."

She shrugged. "It's your birthright, Alexi. I would never ask you to turn that down or stop it. If it's important to you, stand by it."

My mother nodded. "Alexi, no matter what, you'll be a prince. But Jean Claude and other advisers have always suggested that you make the best choice as successor. I've always said I wouldn't choose. And Xander, you have always been who you wanted to be. I don't want to take that away. So, both of you, tell me what you need."

I knew what my brother wanted, and it wasn't the throne. Early on, he'd shunned everything he could from both of our parents. He didn't go into business like my dad, and he didn't listen to any of the royal nonsense Jean Claude had tried to hammer down our throats. All he wanted to do was to be a photographer.

Xander's gaze swung to mine. "Alexi, let's face it, little brother. While you are the better choice, I know that you don't want this."

The relief washed through me. "No, I don't. After what happened last time with Abbie, I couldn't deal with the possibility again."

"Oh, why don't you let me decide what I can deal with?" Abbie said.

I kissed her on the forehead. "Look, I know you can handle it, but I don't *want* to be king. I don't want that power and responsibility. It's not really for me. I don't want to rule. I also know that I failed to protect you once. The way they're going to rake you over the coals, I'm not doing it."

"The only reason people have raked me over the coals was because of the whole Gemma situation. Things are different now."

"Yes, you're my wife. But still, the public gets less than noble when they're faced with someone different. What the press would say about you... I would kill them. And I don't want the throne. I just want you. That's all I ever wanted."

Her dark gaze met mine. "If that's what you say, well then, fair enough. I stand behind you one hundred percent. But if you do want this, say so." She glanced at Xander too. "The same goes for you. Neither one of you needs to fall on the sword. Imani and I are strong enough to handle whatever you want."

Xander stood. "In that case it's settled. Alexi, you're going to be a prince for the rest of your life. I'll step in. Mum, I'll do it."

Imani's brows popped. "You will?"

I echoed her sentiment. "Xan, are you sure?"

He nodded. "Yeah. Absolutely."

I studied him. Our whole lives, he'd wanted freedom. He had escaped to the place that he felt safest. Behind the camera. But suddenly, he was volunteering to be in the public eye?

My mum nodded. "Well, it looks like I'm going to be queen."

"It certainly does look that way, doesn't it?" I muttered.

Later that night, while a whole team of advisers hunkered down in my mother's office, trying to identify the best course of action for a coronation and all the pomp and circumstance that went with it, I found my brother in the study. "What happened to Imani?"

"Apparently, my baby is draining her. She's exhausted. She went to bed. You know, with a cookie in her hand." He did an imitation of my sister-in-law double fisting cookies and wiping crumbs off her chest. It was spot on. It seemed my soon-to-be niece had a sweet tooth.

I couldn't help but chuckle. "Well, I mean, she's growing a human."

"Yeah, but I just happen to know that cookie is going to make her violently ill come the morning."

"Yeah, there's that."

He frowned. "Where's your better half?"

"She got her camera. She's photographing the pow wow in the study. The making of a queen."

Xander chuckled. "Yeah, she was my student, after all."

"Any opportunity to take a photo."

He studied me. "Are you sure you're okay stepping down?"

I nodded. "Yeah, mate. I don't want this. Ruling, it's going to be awful. Which makes me wonder why you want it."

He frowned. "What do you mean? I get to be a prince and one day a king. What's not to love?"

I studied him. "You love Imani. You don't want that for her."

"I love you too. And I don't want this for you."

I knew he was doing this to take care of me. "Xan, I can take care of myself."

"I know. But maybe it's time for me to step up. I could do a lot of good."

"You could. But I've never known you as someone who craves power."

"I don't. I just know that this is what mum wants. And this is something you *don't* want. So, for once, I'm stepping up. And you still get to be a prince. I promise, if mum ever steps down and I become king, I'll be just."

I rolled my eyes. "Yeah. Something tells me that term is going to be all in your head."

He grinned. "Who, me? Never."

♛

Xander

I had bloody lost it.

I knew the moment the words were out of my mouth.

I was going to be my mother's successor. I was clearly mad.

So why did you do it?

Because I knew that Alexi couldn't. My brother had already carried too much. Held on to too much. Worried about too much. So it was time for me to be a big brother for once. Our relationship had always been flipped for some reason, now was my chance to even the score. I knew he was the preferred prince. But still, I could at least offer something.

Imani leaned over in the seat, her hand on my thigh. "Penny for your thoughts?"

I couldn't help it; I was always cheeky. "Why don't you slide your hand up and you'll get more than a penny."

She did and paused just before she hit pay dirt. "Talk first, sex later, remember?"

I couldn't help but smile. "Hey, I think you have that reversed."

"No, you've been quiet since yesterday."

"Look, I don't want you to worry about that. I've got it under control."

"I know you do. But still, you volunteering, falling on the sword like that? What's going on?"

I shrugged. I didn't want to talk about it. I made a right turn, going as slow as I could possibly manage in the car. It was a Pagani Huayra. It was a super car, but I had precious cargo on board.

She rolled her eyes. "First of all, Xander, drive like a normal person, okay? It annoys me when you drive slow. I might as well take the tube."

"Um, hello, my wife is carrying a princess of Nomea in that sizeable belly."

She slid me a narrow-eyed glare. "It's ridiculous in this expensive sports car. Either drive it how it's meant to be driven or don't bother."

I coughed. "Gosh, when did you get so bossy?"

"I think the phrase you're looking for is assertive. And don't deflect. Are you really okay with this?"

I nodded my head. I didn't really have a choice. "Of course, I'm okay with this. This is what I want. And I know we probably should have talked about it first, but things were moving a little quickly."

Her hazel eyes narrowed at me. "That's not what I'm worried about, Xander. I just know that this would be stressful for you. And I'm wondering what you're going through."

"I'm not going through anything. All I want is for you and tiny blueberry in there to be safe and happy. And I'm going to do everything I can to make sure that happens."

"I know that." She took my hand and placed it on her belly. "And I'm trying to make sure that you're mentally safe and happy. So talk to me."

I knew her. She wasn't going to let this go. "I knew Alexi couldn't do it. And Abbie couldn't go through that scrutiny again."

Instead of being annoyed or hurt, or being angry, she gave me a soft smile. "And you're protecting Abbie?"

"I don't know. Maybe. They're my family. Why shouldn't I protect them just like I'll protect you?"

"Oh sweetheart, when are you going to learn? You, Xander Chase, the man, are all I need. You are all blueberry needs. Maybe you don't make choices about the future unless you really want to make those choices. I just want to make sure that you stay nice and centered."

"I am. This could be good for you. Your career, your sister, everything. I know what I'm doing."

She studied me. "Whatever you want to do, I'm behind you. Until I get too fat to really pull that off, and then you'll have to stand behind me. But you get the idea."

I smiled at her. At the light, I leaned over and gave her a kiss. "I love you."

She smiled. "I know."

The light turned yellow then green and I eased forward. Up ahead, I saw two children playing with a ball and I knew how it was going to go. I deliberately kept my speed slow as I rolled past the intersection because sure enough, out came the ball and the younger of the two boys that were playing ran out without any kind of thought.

He skidded to a stop about five feet in front of me. And then he held up a hand in thanks as he gave me a bucktooth grin. All I could do was shake my head as he ran off to join his friend.

One day soon, I was going to have a child. One that I would protect with my life. And saying yes to being a prince would give me everything I needed to make that happen. I'd be able to protect my child in all the ways that I'd wanted to be protected.

It was the sole reason I'd said yes.

Imani thought it was about Alexi or even Abbie, but really, it was all about her and our child. I would do anything for them. Even if it meant—

The only warning before the glass shattered on Imani's side of the car was the hair on my arm standing at attention. Before I knew what was happening, pieces of glass cut the side of my face. Imani's long hair whipped about, and then she screamed.

That scream pierced my soul. There was another crack. More screams. People on the street were running. Even as I swerved the car to a stop, another crack rang out, and the windshield shattered into a million little pieces.

I threw my body over Imani. "Are you okay? Baby, are you all right?"

She didn't answer. I glanced down at her, and that's when I saw the blood. Too much blood, not cuts and scrapes like I could feel on my face, but all over her chest. Someone had shot my wife. All I could do was scream as the cold numbness seeped into my bones.

Someone had shot my wife, and I was going to kill them.

Find out what happens to Xander in Royal Playboy...

⚜

THANK you for reading LONDON SOUL! I hope you enjoyed the London Royal Duet. Now find out if Xander's wife and child survive the royal assassination attempt.

Do you like your playboys, alpha, possessive and broken inside? Meet Xander Chase.

Before her, pussy came easy.

For the first time in my life, I've met a woman who wants nothing to do with me. But I need her to claim vengeance. I'll do what I have to to possess her.

Order Royal Playboy now so you don't miss it!

And you can read Zia and Theo's story in Bodyguard to the Billionaire right now! Three words, Royal, Billionaire, Twins! A bodyguard who knows how to handle her weapons and Royal intrigue that will have you wondering who the killer is! Find out what happens when a filthy, rich billionaire hires a body double, but the simple plan goes awry. **One-click Bodyguard to the Billionaire now!**

> "... *Sinfully sexy. ...A nail-chewing heart-pumping suspense. It was a complete entertainment package."* --***PP's Bookshelf Blog***

Meet a cocky, billionaire prince that goes undercover in Cheeky Royal! He's a prince with a secret to protect. The last distraction he can afford is his gorgeous as sin new neighbor. His secrets could get them killed, but still, he can't stay away...

Read Cheeky Royal for FREE now!

Turn the page for an excerpt from Cheeky Royal...

UPCOMING BOOKS

Royal Playboy
Playboy's Heart
Big Ben
The Benefactor
For Her Benefit

"You make a really good model. I'm sure dozens of artists have volunteered to paint you before."

He shook his head. "Not that I can recall. Why? Are you offering?"

I grinned. "I usually do nudes." Why did I say that? It wasn't true. Because you're hoping he'll volunteer as tribute.

He shrugged then reached behind his back and pulled his shirt up, tugged it free, and tossed it aside. "How is this for nude?"

Fuck. Me. I stared for a moment, mouth open and looking like an idiot. Then, well, I snapped a picture. Okay fine, I snapped several. "Uh, that's a start."

He ran a hand through his hair and tussled it, so I snapped several of that. These were romance-cover gold. Getting into it, *he started posing for me, making silly faces. I got closer to him, snapping more close-ups of his face. That incredible face.*

Then suddenly he went deadly serious again, the intensity in his eyes going harder somehow, sharper. Like a razor. "You look nervous. I thought you said you were used to nudes."

I swallowed around the lump in my throat. "Yeah, at school whenever we had a model, they were always nude. I got used to it."

He narrowed his gaze. "Are you sure about that?"
Shit. He could tell. "Yeah, I am. It's just a human form. Male. Female. No big deal."

His lopsided grin flashed, and my stomach flipped. Stupid traitorous body...and damn him for being so damn good looking. I tried to keep the lens centered on his face, but I had to get several of his abs, for you know...research.
But when his hand rubbed over his stomach and then slid to the button on his jeans, I gasped, "What are you doing?"
"Well, you said you were used doing nudes. Will that make you more comfortable as a photographer?"

I swallowed again, unable to answer, wanting to know what he was doing, how far he would go. And how far would I go?

The button popped, and I swallowed the sawdust in my mouth. I snapped a picture of his hands.

Well yeah, and his abs. So sue me. He popped another button, giving me a hint of the forbidden thing I couldn't have. I kept snapping away. We were locked in this odd, intimate game of chicken. I swung the lens up to capture his face. His gaze was slightly hooded. His lips parted...turned on. I stepped back a step to capture all of him. His jeans loose, his feet bare. Sitting on the stool, leaning back slightly and giving me the sex face, because that's what it was—God's honest truth—the sex face. And I was a total goner.

"You're not taking pictures, Len." His voice was barely above a whisper.

"Oh, sorry." I snapped several in succession. Full body shots, face shots, torso shots. There were several torso shots. I wanted to fully capture what was happening.
He unbuttoned another button, taunting me, tantalizing me. Then he reached into his jeans, and my gaze snapped to meet his. I wanted to say something. Intervene in some way...help maybe...ask him what he was doing. But I couldn't. We were locked in a game that I couldn't break free from. Now I wanted more. I wanted to know just how far he would go.

Would he go nude? Or would he stay in this half-undressed state, teasing me, tempting me to do the thing that I shouldn't do?

I snapped more photos, but this time I was close. I was looking down on him with the camera, angling so I could see his perfectly sculpted abs as they flexed. His hand was inside his jeans. From the bulge, I knew he was touching himself. And then I snapped my gaze up to his face.

Sebastian licked his lip, and I captured the moment that tongue met flesh.

Heat flooded my body, and I pressed my thighs together to abate the ache. At that point, I was just snapping photos, completely in the zone, wanting to see what he might do next.

"Len..."

"Sebastian." My voice was so breathy I could barely get it past my lips.

"Do you want to come closer?"

"I--I think maybe I'm close enough?"

His teeth grazed his bottom lip. "Are you sure about that? I have another question for you."

I snapped several more images, ranging from face shots to shoulders, to torso. Yeah, I also went back to the hand-around-his-dick thing because...wow. "Yeah? Go ahead."

"Why didn't you tell me about your boyfriend 'til now?"

Oh shit. "I—I'm not sure. I didn't think it mattered. It sort of feels like we're supposed to be friends." Lies all lies.

He stood, his big body crowding me. "Yeah, friends..."

I swallowed hard. I couldn't bloody think with him so close. His scent assaulted me, sandalwood and something that was pure Sebastian wrapped around me, making me weak. Making me tingle as I inhaled his scent. Heat throbbed between my thighs, even as my knees went weak. "Sebastian, wh—what are you doing?"

"

Proving to you that we're not friends. Will you let me?"
He was asking my permission. I knew what I wanted to say. I understood what was at stake. But then he raised his hand and traced his knuckles over my cheek, and a whimper escaped.

His voice went softer, so low when he spoke, his words were more like a rumble than anything intelligible. "Is that you telling me to stop?"

Seriously, there were supposed to be words. There were. But somehow I couldn't manage them, so like an idiot I shook my head.

His hand slid into my curls as he gently angled my head. When he leaned down, his lips a whisper from mine, he whispered, "This is all I've been thinking about."

Read Cheeky Royal now!

NANA MALONE READING LIST

Looking for a few Good Books? Look no Further

FREE

Sexy in Stilettos

Game Set Match

Shameless

Before Sin

Cheeky Royal

Royals
Royals Undercover

Cheeky Royal

Cheeky King

Royals Undone

Royal Bastard

Bastard Prince

<u>Royals United</u>
Royal Tease
Teasing the Princess

<u>Royal Elite</u>

The Heiress Duet
Protecting the Heiress
Tempting the Heiress

The Prince Duet
Return of the Prince
To Love a Prince

The Bodyguard Duet
Billionaire to the Bodyguard
The Billionaire's Secret

<u>London Royals</u>

London Royal Duet
London Royal
London Soul

Playboy Royal Duet
Royal Playboy
Playboy's Heart

The Donovans Series

Come Home Again (Nate & Delilah)
Love Reality (Ryan & Mia)
Race For Love (Derek & Kisima)
Love in Plain Sight (Dylan and Serafina)
Eye of the Beholder – (Logan & Jezzie)
Love Struck (Zephyr & Malia)

London Billionaires Standalones

Mr. Trouble (Jarred & Kinsley)
Mr. Big (Zach & Emma)
Mr. Dirty(Nathan & Sophie)

The Shameless World

Shameless

Shameless
Shameful
Unashamed

Force
Enforce

Deep
Deeper

Before Sin
Sin
Sinful

Brazen

Still Brazen

The Player
Bryce

Dax

Echo

Fox

Ransom

Gage

The In Stilettos Series
Sexy in Stilettos (Alec & Jaya)

Sultry in Stilettos (Beckett & Ricca)

Sassy in Stilettos (Caleb & Micha)

Strollers & Stilettos (Alec & Jaya & Alexa)

Seductive in Stilettos (Shane & Tristia)

Stunning in Stilettos (Bryan & Kyra)

~~~

In Stilettos Spin off
Tempting in Stilettos (Serena & Tyson)

Teasing in Stilettos (Cara & Tate)

Tantalizing in Stilettos (Jaggar & Griffin)

Love Match Series
*Game Set Match (Jason & Izzy)

Mismatch (Eli & Jessica)

ABOUT NANA MALONE

USA Today Best Seller, Nana Malone's love of all things romance and adventure started with a tattered romantic suspense she "borrowed" from her cousin.

It was a sultry summer afternoon in Ghana, and Nana was a precocious thirteen. She's been in love with kick butt heroines ever since. With her overactive imagination, and channeling her inner Buffy, it was only a matter a time before she started creating her own characters.

Now she writes about sexy royals and smokin' hot bodyguards when she's not hiding her tiara from Kidlet, chasing a puppy who refuses to shake without a treat, or begging her husband to listen to her latest hair-brained idea.

Made in the USA
Middletown, DE
26 December 2021

57016165R00139